Appointment
with
Unreality

Penelope May

to Denyse —
Thank you for
coming to the reading.
I hope you enjoy the
book.

Allegra May

© 2019 by Penelope May.
All rights reserved. No part of this book may be reproduced or transmitted in any form or by any means, electronic or mechanical, including photocopying, recording, or by any information storage and retrieval system, without permission in writing from the copyright owner.

Print ISBN: 978-1-7330963-0-0
Ebook ISBN: 978-1-7330963-1-7
Library of Congress Control Number: 2019908280

Published by
Kai Press
York, ME 03909
kaipress.com

Produced by
Great Life Press
Rye, New Hampshire 03870
www.greatlifepress.com

This is a work of fiction. Names, characters, places and incidents either are the product of the author's imagination or are used fictitiously, and any resemblance to any actual persons or events is entirely coincidental. Although some Maine locales are named, factual liberties have been taken to support the events of the story.

This book is dedicated to my early readers:
Carolyn, Kay, Deborah, Andrea,
Cathy, and Kaer.

On the Cover

NGC 300 Composite Image: This color composite image of galaxy NGC 300 combines visible-light with ultraviolet views from NASA's Galaxy Evolution Explorer (GALEX).
Credit: NASA/JPL-Caltech/OCIW

Contents

From wonder into wonder
Existence opens.

Laotzu, 550 BC, translated by Witter Bynner

Entry Point

I lay on my back in *shavasana*, legs outstretched, arms weightless at my side, in the relaxation pose of my yoga practice. It was early August and the window was open, causing a faint drift of air over me. I settled into the floor, noticing how quiet it was in Somerville this afternoon. Sounds from the traffic below blended into the meditative music on my phone, and I heard the light click of Rayna coming upstairs.

I began my ocean breathing, churning the air in my throat into the sound of a wave sliding over wet sand. It was a trance-like breath, guaranteed to lift me into a floating state. I let go of the hardness of the floor and the tones of the music, allowing my mind to wander away from my physical body. In this expanded state I liked to imagine my mind could go out into the universe and mingle with whatever might be out there, perhaps to bring back some astonishing discovery.

It was a silly game for me to play, because I was a realist and inclined to pessimism. I'd worked as a counselor in community mental health, where the realities of poverty and social neglect fit my view of the essential injustice of society. All my life the needs of the disadvantaged had tainted my personal happiness—who was I to be happy when they suffered? Not that I hadn't been fortunate and comfortable while I lived a life of service.

Now that I was retired, I'd allowed some whimsy into my routines. In this part of my yoga practice I pretended to flirt with the unreasonable. Sometimes I remembered these excursions into the universe as full of movement and density, like threading my way through a dense crowd of people. Sometimes I fell asleep and remembered nothing.

Eyes closed and drifting, I was vaguely aware that Rayna had laid herself against my side, because she loved body contact. A lightning-fast hunting dog, she had the grace of a cat and fur the color of midnight. Five years before she had arrived as a little puppy, into a house without kids or husband. We formed a bond like no other, and midway through my sixties, she was my last and best companion.

Inside the dream space my mind stirred, lured by something it recognized. Where there had been music on the radio, a buzz of static attracted my attention. I accepted this, allowing my mind to slide away from the sound until it became faint as mist. But the static grew again, insisting on being heard. In time I could pick out words.

Listen. Listen, the static said.

I let the words rest in my mind. Gradually I became aware the words had changed. *Will you help me?* they asked.

I let this request rest as well, and after a while it seemed my heart had agreed that I would. Then came a period of quiet static while I sank towards sleep. The last words I heard were spoken in sorrow: *There will be horror and pain. I am so sorry to use you like this.*

When I woke up some time later, the radio was playing music again and the street noise murmured away. Rayna stood and stretched, waiting for me to sit up, cross my legs, and bow out of the session. I lay on the floor, trying to feel myself floating beyond the ceiling, but nothing remained of the space I'd been in.

Except the words. I remembered the words all right.

The Voice

The next day I worried about the words in the static. Certainly I'd been asleep and dreaming, because there's no such thing as static from a digital phone. The buzz of static belonged to the baseball broadcasts on the car radios of my childhood.

But this static had carried words, words that were coherent and convincing. They asked something of me, which I had agreed to—stupidly it now seemed to me, since apparently whatever it was involved pain and suffering. The sorrow of the last words hung over me all day, as if a close friend had shared a personal tragedy.

It seemed ridiculous that the dream had a stubborn reality I just couldn't shake. As a mental health professional, I was well acquainted with the mind, its dreams, and its abnormal states. It made no sense that I couldn't distinguish between an obvious dream and a real life experience. The more I tried to understand the dream, the more confused I became, until by the end of the day I resolved to put the whole thing aside, to be revisited at a later time.

August went on, with tomatoes to pick in the back yard and walks to take in the woods with Rayna. I did a series of watercolor paintings, went to my drawing group, and continued to practice yoga, although somehow I never had time for the *shavasana* pose.

The last Saturday in August I was up at sunrise for an agility trial. I'd loaded the car the night before and Rayna knew exactly where we were going. She bounded into the back of the car, ears up and eyes gleaming. At a distance she could be mistaken for a black fox: sharp, pointed ears, narrow muzzle, slim legs and feet. Up close she was a different animal.

She had a lean, powerful body, with a deep chest and muscular back legs that let her spring straight up in the air from a standing position. Her ruff was short and stiff on her strong neck, and her eyes were so dark they blended with the black of her face, giving her a mysterious expression. When relaxed, her thick tail curved over her back in the shape of a sickle. Rayna was a Kai Ken, an ancient breed of dog from the landlocked mountains of Japan, bred to hunt bear and wild boar. Kai are considered a national treasure in Japan, and with good reason. They are brave and intelligent hunters, who will be your equal partner for as long as they live.

As we headed north on the interstate, I felt the same tense energy I used to feel in the hours before I ran a triathlon. Although today might look easier than a triathlon, it had its own special challenges. Instead of sustained exertion over time, today would consist of a series of thirty- to sixty-second dashes around a complex course, with the handler directing the dog through a complicated set of obstacles. Keeping your wits about you was essential, and so was staying in touch with your canine teammate, who was likely to design her own course the moment you broke your connection with her.

Driving from the highway onto country roads, eventually we ended up on a long dirt track running through the deserted fields behind a fairground. The trial site was at the far end, in an area marked off by a chain link fence lined with the RVs and campers that had spent the night. Two big gates opened onto a lane that ran past two huge agility rings. Along the other side of the lane, cars and pickup trucks parked side by side facing the rings. Easy-ups, folding chairs, crates, handlers, and dogs surrounded the rings at the requisite distance from the fencing.

It was still cool, so I parked the car behind the others that faced the advanced ring where Rayna would run. In a few hours I'd have to move the car to the shade under the trees several hundred feet away, but for now we could watch the ring while we waited for our classes. Telling Rayna to "keep the car," I went to check in. The first course of the day was already set up and handlers were walking it, checking their course maps, and considering their approaches to obstacles. Occasionally small groups of people would cluster to discuss how to handle a sequence.

The first class was called "snooker," a complex game involving four red jumps and a series of numbered obstacles with ascending point values—the harder the obstacle, the higher its points. At the beginning of the game, the dog must first take a red jump and then one of the point obstacles, and do this red jump-obstacle combination three times using three different red jumps. The red jumps are scattered over the course, and a mistake anywhere in this first sequence ends the run, so it's the handler's job to design a fast but workable sequence. Assuming all goes well in the opening, the dog must then do all the point obstacles in order, earning points until the course time ends.

The last obstacle in the course earned the highest points, and in this case it was two obstacles to be taken in sequence: a double jump followed by weave poles. Weave poles are difficult because the dog has to weave through them with speed and accuracy, and rhythm helps. When the fastest dogs do the weaves, you see their bodies twitch back and forth and hear the poles rattle, and it's all over in two or three seconds. Rayna wasn't that fast, but fast enough, and she rarely missed a pole.

The double jump and weave poles were located at the bottom right of the course, and conveniently opposite them were two red jumps, forming a rough circle. If you could circle through once doing a red jump, the double, and the weaves, and then circle again doing the other red jump, the double, and the weaves, you could earn a pile of points. On the other hand, if your dog took the two red jumps back to back, the game was over. There was also the problem of getting to a third red jump at the back of the course, in order to finish the beginning sequence. Walking the course, I wondered if I could pull this off.

As we waited at the gate for our turn to run, my pulse was up and my stomach tight. To keep both of us happy, I leaned down and offered Rayna my face. She stood with her front paws on my knee and we nuzzled, nose to cheek. When I straightened, she hopped down and gave me a grin, letting me know she was ready.

I set her up in front of the first of the two red jumps on the right, told her to wait, and backed out onto the course. The trick was to have her take the first red jump and ignore the second, so I kept my back firmly to the second one.

"Ok," I released her, and with an avid look on her face, front paws together and body out flat, she went over the first red jump. I pointed her to come around and take the double jump, calling "Weave!" before she jumped so she'd be ready for the weaves. She sailed over the double and danced through the weaves, and by now I was between the second red jump and the double, calling her over the second jump and on to the double again. She recognized the pattern, took the double and the weaves, and I was already moving toward the heart of the course and the third red jump.

When Rayna was younger, I could trot to strategic places in the course to direct her. Now, with arthritis in my back, there was no more trotting, but while I was getting older, she was learning to work at a distance. When I focused and my timing was good, it was as if she was inside my mind and seeing through my eyes.

"Out!" I called, to tell her to take the red jump ten feet in front of her, and before she jumped, "Right!" so she would bend to the right as she jumped. "Out!" I called as she landed, thrusting my palm out toward a numbered jump twenty feet from her. She understood and ran out to take that jump and complete the first part of the game. I was exhilarated, now we only had to follow the numbered obstacles in sequence and accumulate points. It was a long course but it flowed, and I kept near the center while she gobbled up the obstacles around the edge. When she leaped on the table to stop the clock, I shouted praise to her. She frisked out of the ring, and the two of us ran back to the car for her special treats.

Not many runs go as well as this one had, and it felt like my happiness would last the whole day. We walked around the trial site to unwind, then went back to the car to wait for the next class. This was an easy follow-the-numbers type of course, and after it I moved the car over to the trees and set up an exercise pen in the shade. Staking the corners, I put Rayna inside and went back to the ring to work as a volunteer.

My volunteer job was bar setting, a simple task of moving the jump bars to the correct height or resetting a bar that was knocked down. Most of the time I sat inconspicuously by the side of the ring, enjoying the sight of dogs running the course. A small Papillon made me smile as it hustled along the long plank of the dog walk, its big butterfly ears bouncing.

As the Pap paused before the down ramp, its eyes met mine,

and something horrible happened. A wave of rage swept through me, bringing me to my feet and twisting my face into what must have been a furious mask. I could see the little dog's panic, and heard it squeal as it fled down the ramp. My hands convulsed with the urge to break its neck and I stepped forward, when an explosion of hysterical barking rang from the trees—Rayna, her bark singing out as if a bear stood right in front of her.

I recoiled, choking. She barked without pause and spectators began glancing uncomfortably toward the trees. As I fled toward the gate of the ring, I was aware of approving looks from people who thought I was running to stop that crazy barking. Actually, I was running away from my own panic and toward the sound I trusted most. I wove through the parked cars and ran across the grass, until I tumbled on the ground in front of Rayna's pen. She went quiet as soon as she saw me and, truthfully, I felt safe with her. Nausea came over me and passed, and I rolled on my back to gaze at the tops of the trees. In her pen, Rayna lay down confidently to wait.

After a while I considered the ants and bugs whose territory I'd invaded, and got to my feet. I let Rayna out of the pen so I could be with her, and the two of us sat in the back of the car while I struggled to find the cause of this rage and fear. A sudden drop in blood pressure? Something I ate? Was I coming off the high of the morning?

Thank god Rayna barked. It seemed like no one saw my twisted face or guessed I was a monster ready to kill. But the thing was, I liked the little dog. And even if I didn't, I wasn't capable of killing a dog, much less with my own hands. That is, I thought I wasn't, but now I wasn't sure. The blast of rage was like being possessed, if there was such a thing.

My thoughts circled around once more to find an explanation. Maybe I was hungry, or just tired out. After more ineffective deliberation, I decided hunger and fatigue were the closest I was going to get to an explanation. Stroking Rayna's black velvet ears, I rested my face against her neck, until eventually I felt steady enough to get out of the car and go look for lunch.

We did one run in the afternoon, for which I had no heart and Rayna didn't qualify. It didn't matter, because by then I was sure there was something urgent I needed to do at home, although I couldn't say exactly what it was. I pulled Rayna from the last two classes and spent the drive home rethinking the whole episode. Clearly she barked to stop me from attacking the little dog, but the mystery was how, way over by the trees, she knew what I was thinking. Surely she couldn't feel my intention across several hundred feet.

At home I was content to sit outside in the sun and close my eyes, with no thought of the trial we'd left early. By the time I got up to go in and make dinner, something was bothering me, something about the trial. I'd been tired and hungry and Rayna had started to bark, so I ran to her pen and fell on the ground. But I was grateful she'd barked, because once I was out of the ring I could go eat lunch. This didn't feel like an adequate description of the morning, but I did remember that the first class had been pretty great. What eluded me entirely was why I'd bailed on the last two classes.

That night I went to sleep full of unnamed concerns, slept poorly, and woke up when rain and wind arrived with dawn. Getting up to close the window, I noticed how vulnerable Rayna looked, curled on my bed in her ball of sleep. A sudden fear prodded me, but my brain protested it was too tired for such crap and I went back to bed, to dream agitated dreams filled with words spilling onto the ground.

Two hours later my sleep-clogged brain woke up, driven by a compulsion to write down what it could remember of the words. Instead of eating breakfast, I sat in the kitchen making a list:

For good
Care
Your spirit
Protect
Winter beach
Danger
Hide
Too many
Hunts
Not safe

There seemed to be more words and phrases than these, but

I supposed they'd sunk into the mire of my unconscious. All day I carried around the small weight of these phrases, sometimes checking my list to remind myself of what they were. The first five phrases seemed positive, the second five threatening, and taken all together they meant nothing.

I waited until late afternoon to do yoga, hoping the practice would center me for the evening. But as I stepped on the mat, my mind cried out, *Not safe!* I stood still and breathed deeply to calm myself, because of course it was safe. *Hunts*, went though my mind, and the single word unexpectedly expanded to *It hunts me.* At that I stepped off the mat and went to sit on the couch. *Not safe* and *It hunts me*, if true, did not bode well.

Although these were only words from a dream, it seemed oddly important to pay attention. Of course I knew dreams were a product of the unconscious, delivering messages that had as little truth as folktales and bible stories. Some anxiety must have woken me at dawn (the blowing rain, for instance) and then fed my fear after I went back to sleep, producing this string of words. But I knew it was the end of yoga for today, because like it or not, my attention had been hijacked. Inviting Rayna to keep me company, I took the list downstairs to my office where it was easier to concentrate.

Beginning with the phrase, *Winter beach*, I let my imagination play. Picturing an empty beach worn bare by January winds, I decided the beach should be a place where no one would bother us and Rayna could run free. Abruptly, the phrase in my mind turned into *Find the winter beach.*

So this was going to be a word hunt. Evening came, as I slowly went through the list, visualizing a phrase and waiting for its meaning to develop. As the list filled in, I rearranged the sentences over and over, until I arrived at this:

> *It hunts me.*
> *I hide in your thoughts.*
> *You protect me.*
> *I am a power for good.*
> *We are in danger.*

Here is not safe.
Too many people. Too difficult to manage.
Find the winter beach.
Keep your spirit with you.
Take care.

I took this list to the kitchen, where I fed Rayna her long-delayed supper and ate a sandwich I didn't taste. It made a fairly consistent story, one that I was pretty sure came from a source outside myself. Something that was being hunted was hiding in my thoughts. It was a power for good and I protected it. Both of us were in danger, because there were too many people here and it was too difficult to stay safe. I'd better go find a beach for the winter and I should keep my spirit with me, whatever that meant. The sad thing was that the story sounded insane.

Shivering in the August heat, I put on a sweater and still felt cold. I thought of friends I might call to talk this over with, but then I hesitated. I could say I had a dream that told me I was in danger and should get out of Boston for the winter. My friends would ask what kind of danger and I would have to tell them the bit about a thing in my mind that was hiding from a hunter—which was not something I'd seriously say to anyone I knew. It wasn't even real, it was a dream, a spooky story from my unconscious.

So instead I drank tea and persuaded myself that maybe I had a need to spend the winter away from the city. It was intriguing to think of leaving Somerville with its hints of danger, and the next day I got on the web to browse Midcoast Maine winter rentals. I saw pretty houses with sunlit decks, kitchens shining with white cabinets, and many pastel quilts spread over queen beds, but nothing I wanted. In my childhood, my family had left New York city to spend summers in run-down cottages on bluffs overlooking the ocean. The house I was looking for was darker and older.

After a while I shut down the computer and, longing to return to an ordinary world, put myself back into a life where there were no such things as blasts of rage against cute little dogs. I was convinced that my problems stemmed from being overtired, a state which caused me to have weird dreams. But anxiety often woke me at night and eventually I did become overtired. Doing yoga always seemed like a bad idea, and I didn't enter Rayna in any more agility trials.

———

Two weeks into September I had a nightmare. I was climbing a steep trail up the side of what might be a great canyon. It was sunset and the bright sun hurt my eyes. Under me was a drop of a thousand feet to the desert floor, and I could barely move my legs from the fear of falling. I put a foot down on the trail and it slipped in loose shale. Losing my balance, I snatched hold of a small twiggy bush, but its roots pulled out of the red soil. I was falling backwards into nothing, impossibly falling, my terror increasing with each moment, and still I didn't hit the ground. I woke up with such awful pain in my chest, I thought I was having a heart attack.

Standing over me on the bed, Rayna began to lick my face energetically, which I guess was her version of CPR. I shoved her away so I could breathe, then tried to apologize by hugging her. Calmly, she turned once in a tight circle and curled up against my side. Lying in the dark, with an arm around Rayna to hold her tight against me, for the first time I remembered the events of last August clearly. There'd been a voice in the static, I'd been possessed by rage at the trial, and the words I'd dreamt were undoubtedly true. At that moment, I realized my rage at the trial was the rage of the hunter that hunted the thing in my head.

Afraid to breathe, afraid to move, I tried to sense if the hunter could be anywhere near. Finally the darkness in the room became oppressive and I had to sit up and turn on the light. That was better, but I was still frightened and my phone told me it was only three thirty. I got up, dressed, and went down to my office, keeping Rayna close because there was no way I'd be separated from her now. On the web I found what I wanted almost immediately, a little two story house with dark wood shingles, sitting at the corner of a lot on the edge of an evergreen forest. At the front of the house was a shallow porch with windows on either side of the door, and on the forest side was a driveway with a short set of stairs leading to a back door.

———

Interior pictures showed rooms with dark brown trim and shiny wooden floors. The living room had an older stuffed couch, two used leather chairs, and a worn looking Oriental rug. Across the hall was a dining room with a large oak table, and next to it the kitchen, with lime green cabinets and what must be the back door on the driveway. The downstairs bathroom had a cast iron bathtub with big iron feet, and in the front hall, a dark brown staircase went up to the second floor bedrooms. It was a sweet 1920s summer house where children must have run barefoot up and down the stairs all day long, and I couldn't imagine how it came to be listed as a winter rental. I sent a text to the realtor and, feeling a little safer than before, went with Rayna to doze on the living room couch until the sun came up.

By daylight the nightmare had lost some of its terror, and I puzzled over why I'd been so sure the rage came from the hunter. I was giving the story of a hunter a credibility it didn't deserve, mixing dream with reality until the two were thoroughly confused. How gullible was I? The voice in the static seemed real, the rage had been horribly real, but here I was in my house with my dog, and nothing was wrong. It was possible I was experiencing a sleep disorder that distorted my judgment, so I should be cautious about making abrupt decisions.

The realtor called me around ten, quite pleased to get my text. She didn't comment on the time I sent it and I supposed she must think city people kept all kinds of hours. I described myself as an artist who wanted to abandon the city, to explore the winter countryside with my dog and to paint beach landscapes. Yes, she said, there was a nice little beach for walking, but it could get quite cold out there. That was ok, I could paint winter scenes from inside, I told her, and added it looked like a nice location.

Absolutely, lovely vistas, she assured me. The town got quiet when the tourists left, but there were bigger towns inland. Some town people worked at the state prison, but she didn't think that would interest me very much, and she laughed. I hated prisons and let the joke go by. She said the house was on the western side of town, almost in the country, and of course it had a furnace. She'd be happy to set up oil delivery and snow plowing if I wanted. I could feel the pull of the little house growing stronger as we talked, and that a decision was imminent, sleep disorder or not.

Before I fully committed myself, I called my daughter in California to test the waters.

"Why would you want to go there?" was her first response.

"I don't really know," I answered truthfully. "Maybe I'm bored here."

"Well sure, living alone is boring." This was an old topic between us.

"Emily, I don't want another relationship. I like my freedom too much."

"We can't always have what we want."

I nearly burst out laughing, but got myself in hand. "Honey, I've had years of family life."

"I'm not saying family, I'm saying one other person."

When I didn't reply, she tried another tack. "What do we do about Christmas?"

"Everyone can visit me in Maine. There are three bedrooms upstairs. I'll send you a link to the house, you'll like it."

"What about Rayna's agility, both of you love that. Isn't Portland a little far to drive?"

"I'm not so interested in agility right now."

A pause, and then she asked perceptively, "Are you depressed?"

"It's possible," I admitted. That was the moment I could have said, "Honey, I had a scary thing happen at Rayna's agility trial," or "Honey, I had a horrible dream last night," or even "Honey, I think I might be hearing a voice inside my head." But even with my kids, there was a gap in my trust.

Spirit

Rayna and I moved in early October, the traditional end of tourist season in Maine. Once I made up my mind to move, there was no time for dreams, fears, or unexplained events. Instead of going up to look at the house, I put my faith in the online pictures and signed the lease. My Somerville house was rented to a visiting faculty member with remarkable speed, which I took as a favorable sign. If I'd been thinking clearly, I might have noticed that things were working out a little too easily, but by then I'd decided that Rayna and I were escaping to a safer place. In the next weeks I packed my life into boxes, storing what I didn't need in the garage and taking the rest with me. Finally, I followed the moving truck out of Somerville with the expectation of vacation, as if I was reliving the summers of my childhood.

Three and a half hours later I saw the little house for the first time, sitting staunchly at the corner of its large lawn. It was as cute as any summer cottage my parents had rented, and from then on it was "the cottage" to me. After the movers had unloaded and gone, Rayna and I found the local shopping center to stock up the kitchen. Later we walked around the neighboring streets and I decided it was good to be there.

The last thing I did that night was make up my bed. I lay down, exhausted by the drive up and the move, and glad of the fresh air and utter quiet. All the houses we'd seen on our walk were shut for the winter, and the cottage was isolated at the end of its dark street. I closed my eyes, felt Rayna warm against my back—and heard words, clear and distinct, speaking in my head.

You are here.

I sat up, staring into the blackness, a vast disappointment ballooning around me.

"Who's there?" I challenged the voice, disgusted with it and my stupidity. Of course it would hitch a ride with me, it was in danger too.

It chose not to reply and I was only too glad. The last thing I wanted was conversation. How dare it make itself real here, bringing confusion and danger to my life?

The voice was stronger here than in Somerville, possibly because of the isolation of the cottage. It occurred to me that maybe it could speak more clearly here because we'd left the danger back in Somerville. That would be a good thing, but the bad thing was that I still couldn't account for its presence. Worse, did this mean I'd be inhabited by a voice for the rest of my life? The idea was offensive.

But this voice had its own methods. Gradually a feeling of peace dissolved my concern and I heard Rayna murmur happily in a canine dream of pursuit. In the end I accepted the dark and the silence, and slid under the covers to drift asleep.

My feelings of peace and contentment persisted well into the next day. After our morning walk, Rayna and I rode around town to locate the essentials: town hall, library, and post office. We found them scattered on two main streets, along with a coffee shop and bakery, open now and hopefully for the whole winter. A charming seaside town, I concluded on the way home.

Yet as I climbed the back steps to the kitchen, I could see my mood alter. It was time for lunch but there were boxes of plates and glasses stacked in a corner of the kitchen. Why the hell had I come here if the damn voice was still in my head? I cut the tape on the top box and began taking out each glass, wiping it down, and putting it in the cabinet. It was definitely bad to be hearing words in my head. Ok, it had only been three words stating the obvious (how smart was this voice anyway?), but where there were three, there would be plenty more.

How could I take a voice in my head seriously? I'd been trained in a rational interpretation of the world, so it was impossible to believe in the voice's reality. Yet in spite of that, every experience of the voice felt completely real. Starting on the box of dishes, I wiped them and stacked them on the kitchen table until it was covered. Last night and this morning I'd felt safer and happier than even in the early, happy days of my marriage. But now I was fully awake, anxious, and edgy, and the dishes made a jarring clatter when I pushed them into the cabinets.

When evening came I was mired in self-doubt, but again that night I went to sleep surrounded by a kindness and wisdom greater than anything my small mind could invent. The next days were similar and a pattern soon established itself. By day, it didn't feel sane to be lulled to sleep by something that couldn't exist, and by night I was just grateful for its kindness.

The morning Rayna and I discovered the beach was a happy morning. I knew the beach was north of town and accessible from the cottage through a network of streets. Driving onto the shore road, I looked for a small road that disappeared in the direction of the ocean. The road was hiding between two high bushes, and I followed it to an unpaved parking area that could barely fit half a dozen cars. With Rayna on her long line, we climbed a path from the parking lot and discovered blue ocean to the left and golden marshland to the right.

The path ended at a bluff overlooking the curve of a gray, wind-blown beach. At the north end of the beach was a wild headland of grass and stunted trees, and at the south end I could see a flat ledge of rocks you could walk on if you were careful. Next to the rock ledge the waves rushed in and out, creating a ceaseless tumble of small rocks that made a rattling sound like applause.

The slope from the bluff to the beach was covered by smooth beach rocks, tossed up from the sea in countless winter storms, and climbing down I had to look where I put my feet. Once on the sand, I let Rayna off the line so she could streak toward a lone seagull. It rose in an unconcerned arc and flew out over the water. At least, I decided, this beach was worth coming for.

A week passed as I shuttled between anxious days and peaceful nights, until I began to wake in the mornings with vague recollections of conversation during the night. I felt I knew things about the voice that I hadn't known the day before, although I couldn't say what these things were. Good god, I thought, am I on the way to a breakdown? True, I never heard the malicious, destructive yammering of schizophrenia in my head, but I thought I might be becoming delusional. I considered looking for a therapist in the area, but gave it up as an idea with too many pitfalls, chief among these being, if I was ill what would happen to Rayna?

––––––––

The accident occurred on a chill late October day when the sky was a perfect blue. Rayna and I were out walking a country road that ran west out of town, and we'd just come up on a long field. Across the field, a parade of big, dark birds head-bobbed their way over the yellow grass. Rayna was on her tracking line and immediately plunged into the tall grass at the edge of the field, sending the birds striding away as fast as they could go. I was about to call her when I saw her leap sideways in surprise, recover herself, and continue on after the birds. Setting my feet firmly against the impact when she hit the end of her line, I called loudly to her. She came right back to me and we went on with our walk, but soon I noticed bright red spots dotting the dirt behind her, as she walked at the edge of the road.

I made her stand while I inspected each paw. There was a deep gash in the pad of her front foot, and I set the paw down carefully. We were more than a mile from home and I hadn't seen a car on this road yet, but Kai are athletic and brave, and I guessed we'd make it back ok. Usually, I embraced emergencies as an opportunity to triumph over adversity, a trait that had been useful when I worked in community mental health.

We went slowly, and by the time we got to town I was more than annoyed. What idiots threw glass bottles in the bushes anyway? Rayna was favoring her injured paw and I felt guilty making her walk back. But what choice did I have, here where I knew no one? This thought launched a familiar train of doubts, starting with we never should have come here and ending with of course the voice in my head had never been real. At home, I soaked Rayna's paw and called the vet. By the time I brought her in for the appointment, I felt anxious as well as guilty. In the waiting room, I groused about tourists throwing bottles around the countryside, just like people did in the city.

"Tourists don't use the back roads that much," the vet tech said. "More likely it was high school kids carousing after a game. You know, before the town got the internet. Now they stay home."

We returned to the cottage with Rayna wearing a bright green day-glow bandage around her pure black paw. I was told to rest her and keep the paw dry for a week.

The next morning was one of those miraculously warm days of fall, a flash of heat at the edge of winter. For a moment I was ecstatic that Rayna and I could play on the beach, but then I remembered that she couldn't play until the paw healed. I fed her and walked her around the house a few times before bringing her back in. Now she lay on the kitchen floor, alert to the somber way I was putting on my walking shoes. Her large triangular ears twitched and her black eyes followed me, but she didn't attempt to stand up. Reading me perfectly, she knew I was going for a walk without her.

I ran alternatives through my mind. We could walk to the bluff and sit in the sun, but that wasn't enough walking for me. We could drive around, but I'd still be miserable without a decent walk. I sighed aloud, why was leaving her so hard? I'd be back in half an hour.

"We'll have another walk when I get back, I promise," I told her. I went out the kitchen door, the morning going to pieces around me.

Mornings were usually my best time, because the voice had learned to make sure I slept well. It was disappointing that he—I'd given him a gender—hadn't done a better job this morning. The afternoons were hard enough, with my rational mind assailing me with questions like, "What unresolved trauma does this voice express?" The logical me was becoming more and more certain I'd developed an obsession, which was a lot easier to believe than finding an explanation for the presence of a voice.

I went down the back steps to the driveway and got in the car. I still hadn't told either of my children, first, because the delusion was embarrassing to put into words, and second, because I suspected the mental health system wouldn't deal well with me. If I was misdiagnosed, overmedicated, and hospitalized, would the kids fly Rayna to the west coast where she would run away? Or put her in a kennel here, where she would also run away? Abandoning Rayna was the wall where my hopes always crashed.

For god's sake, I thought, the beach is only five minutes away. I put on my seatbelt and backed out onto the street.

Assuming the voice was real (the crucial assumption), he was in danger from the hunter. But I knew he was concerned about me as well, and even up here I needed to watch out for myself. Except he was very short on the details of how to stay safe. "Always keep your spirit with you," was what he had told me, which was hardly helpful because it made no sense.

––––––––

Walking along the path to the ocean, I appreciated how the marsh grass glowed in morning sun. Occasional white flecks on the far side of the marsh might have been birds against the dark evergreens. When I reached the bluff I was surprised that even on this lovely day the beach was deserted. I wondered if people here ever used the beach to run, or whether running wasn't the fashion when you worked hard all day. Before my arthritis, when I trained for triathlons regularly, an empty beach was an invitation to run until the beat of my breath blotted out all thought. I believed in the therapeutic power of physical exertion and the antidepressant value of a hard run.

I stood on the edge of the bluff, musing that I ought to start practicing yoga again, when sudden terror seized me. The ground under my feet had vanished, along with everything around me. I stood on transparent air and hundreds of feet below me a ruffled blue ocean stretched from horizon to horizon. I realized the solid earth was no more and everything I cherished was gone—Rayna, my children and grandchildren, the beautiful earth, all of it ripped away. There was nothing now but air and ocean.

My heart broke in pieces and I was blind with grief. Stumbling forward, I staggered down the slope until I tripped at the bottom and fell on my knees in the sand.

The sand was hard and chilly. Yes, I was on the beach. Kneeling there, I wiped pointless tears off my face. What the hell just happened? Did I have a stroke? I squinted up at the sun and put my hands over my eyes.

I could feel the sun on the backs of my hands, warm and comfortable. Suddenly, the skin on my hands crackled and seared, smoke and flames bursting out around my knuckles. For a moment I was stunned by pain, then I beat my hands wildly against my legs as fire devoured my fingers. Ramming my hands into the sand, I tried to smother the fire as it crawled up my wrists. Now my face was exposed to the sun and the skin on my cheeks caught fire and began to melt.

Howling, I turned away from the ocean. The sun on my back warmed my shirt and the skin between my shoulder blades ignited. Agony piled on agony, I must have been screaming but I heard nothing. The pain was so great, my body was being overwhelmed. As my throat constricted I doubled over, unable to breathe.

Cold fingers touched my shoulder. An icy hand laid itself on my back, radiating cold. Black sheets of freezing water began to cascade over me, sheet after sheet until I ached with cold. I slid into a glacial lake and swam below the surface, at peace.

Slowly I came back. I was breathing. I was on the sand. Someone was beside me. A hand was on my back. I stayed where I was, shuddering with cold.

Gradually I began to feel the warmth of the air, but I had no intention of moving. Whoever had their hand on my back was in no hurry and waited patiently. My hands, my face, my back screamed with recent burns and finally I had to look. Sitting up slowly, I raised my poor hands in front of my face: no burns, no scars, no marks on them at all. I gently touched my cheeks, which were smooth and intact. The pain receded. It took several tries before my voice worked.

I wheezed, "I was on fire, my skin was burning up!"

At this my rescuer lifted the hand and sat back. I glanced over, it was a young guy around forty, light brown skin, fit looking. His black eyes were shining in an odd way and it crossed my mind he knew something.

Turning to face the water, I tried to steady my racing heart. I had to be careful here, he could call the police at any moment. Obviously I was cracking up. For a while we sat and watched the quiet ocean together.

Finally he asked, "Do you think you should go to the hospital?"

"I seem to be all right," I answered doubtfully.

There was another lengthy pause before he asked, "Does this happen often?" Maybe he was a medic.

"It never happened before. I don't know what happened."

He raised his eyebrows slightly and I looked away to consider my options. He had extinguished the fire, I was pretty sure of that. Did that make him safe to talk to?

When I looked back at him, he offered his hand. "My name's Tomás."

"Lee," I said, taking his. It was the hand he'd put on my back, a regular hand, the color of *café con leche*.

Now he waited, watching me. When it was clear I wasn't going to say or do anything more, he got to his feet.

"You live around here? I'll take you home."

"I have a car," I mumbled, hoping he'd go away. I needed to get home, where I could figure all of this out.

"It's no problem, I'll come back for it," he said, offering a hand to help me up.

I didn't have the will to argue, so I took his hand and attempted to stand. When my knees refused to take my weight, he took my arm over his shoulders and more or less lifted me up the slope. It was strange to be carried like this, a helpless person, because I'd never needed this kind of help before. At the top he encouraged me to try to walk, which I managed. He's a caregiver at a retirement home, I decided, someone skilled at aiding the halt and the lame. In the parking area he opened the passenger door of an old and humble car.

"Keys?" he inquired when I was seated.

I pulled them from my pocket and watched him go over to my car. Looking for money? Drugs? Maybe he was a cop. Or con man. He peered inside the car, shut the door, and came back, as it occurred to me he was checking that we didn't leave behind anything I needed. I clutched the keys he handed me and described how to get back to the cottage. We drove slowly out of the parking area.

As we wound back through the streets, my mind was busy composing a story that would send him happily away as soon as we reached the cottage. I had a mild breakdown this morning, possibly because I left my dog at home—no, that made me sound unstable. I just moved here, I'm overtired, exhausted by the move—too fragile. I tripped and fell down the slope, which triggered a post traumatic episode—possible.

I said as cheerfully as I could, "Thank you for helping me. So stupid, to fall down the bluff!"

He was listening.

"Falling like that, it scared me to death. You see," he was still listening, "I had an incident in the past, a trauma. It involved fire."

He stopped at the stop sign where he would turn left, reached over, and wrapped his hand around my wrist.

"Lee, I saw fire all over your back."

"Bullshit you did—" I whispered, staring helplessly at him. Then I jerked my arm away, with nothing to say for myself.

"It had to be a powerful illusion, for me to see it," he commented to the windshield as he made the turn.

I gazed fiercely out my side window. Look what I got myself into, now how was I going to get rid of this guy?

We were a street away from the cottage when we heard the barking—fierce, outraged, incessant. "Touch me, I'll kill you!" it shouted.

"Rayna!" I cried, grabbing for the dashboard. The danger was real, I realized, it had found me at the beach, and now it had found my dog.

He couldn't have known what was happening, but he floored the gas anyway. When he braked at my front lawn, I tumbled out of the car and scrambled to the front door. The barking raged on while I got the key in the lock and thrust the door open. In the living room a furious black creature leapt from the couch to the rug, sprang straight into the air with vicious snapping teeth, and jumped back to its perch on the couch. All at once I recognized it was Rayna and understood. She was my spirit and I'd left her at home.

"Rayna, leave it!" I cried, terrified she might burst into flames.

With a flick, her attention shifted. She charged the living room window and stood, paws on the sill, head tossing and tail thrashing with every bark. Then she raced into the dining room where she searched every corner, turned from there to dash through the kitchen, then came up the hall and into the living room again.

We watched her check the couch, the chairs, the windows, following instincts bred into generations of hunters. She swept back into the dining room, once more into the kitchen and up the hall, and finally stopped to address us at the front door. The fur stood high on her neck and back, her body trembled with energy, her tail was as stiff as a rod. Clearly she wasn't done with this job.

I got on my knees and she came to me, licking my face anxiously as if I might have been harmed. She looked unhurt and was standing on her bandaged paw, so I guessed she'd survived the mayhem. There were pillows and a blanket strewn across the living room rug. Tomás picked up the blanket, gave it to me, and walked off to the kitchen as if it was his house. I wrapped myself in the blanket and collapsed on the couch, where Rayna immediately joined me.

Dogs Know More Than Us

Tomás drank black tea in one of the leather chairs, while Rayna slept with her head on my lap as if nothing had happened. I wasn't doing as well as she was. Waves of shock passed over me, making my teeth chatter. I'd lost track of the morning's traumas: losing the world and what I loved, the fear and agony of being on fire, Rayna's harrowing bark, and my terror that she might go up in flames. This stranger sat in my living room, as perfectly willing to wait as he had been on the beach.

"Tough morning," he finally observed. When I kept silent, he prompted, "Why don't we talk about it?"

I looked at this guy in running shoes and worn sweatshirt, repeating the time-honored words of a shrink, with no clue who he was or whether I could trust him. He'd helped me on the beach (but what had happened there?) and Rayna appeared to trust him (but what had happened to her?). He was obviously someone who could take charge of a situation, but that wasn't always a good thing. And if he really was a shrink, that wasn't necessarily a good thing either.

He was watching me sympathetically. He'd claimed to see fire on my back, which he said was an illusion. It was true I hadn't been physically burned, but it was another of those experiences that felt outrageously real. Except this morning I couldn't breathe and that was a higher order of threat. I shifted nervously, remembering that the voice had warned me of danger.

Supposing there was real danger, then I really needed to talk to someone about this . . . could I still call it a delusion? But whatever it was, I just didn't know if this was the right guy. Let him go first, I decided.

I asked, "How did you put out the fire?"

"The fire was an illusion." He was surprisingly calm about this.

"Yes, you said that. But how did you stop it, how did you make the cold? I thought I was dying."

"Well," he shrugged, "if you really want to know, I prayed to my Savior to help me heal you."

I couldn't stop myself from making a face. Great, he's a religious nut, now what?

But he smiled tolerantly. "I'm a priest. Praying to Jesus is what we do."

"Really?" I sat straight up, launching Rayna off my lap. She woke up instantly and landed on her feet.

"Is that ok with you?" It was a polite challenge.

"It's—," I hesitated. "I think it's all right."

I wasn't going to tell him I thought religious belief was a backward way of thinking, but I could see advantages to talking with this man. Priests trafficked in the unbelievable, they took angels and demons seriously, and they might not assume I was nuts if I said there was a presence in my mind. Plus they were bound by privileged communication.

"Do you have a church around here?" I fished, but there was his Latino name and appearance. "Or are you visiting?"

"Yeah, you can tell I'm not a local guy." He had a playful smile. "I'm on loan from Chicago, serving at the state prison."

"By choice?" I asked, skeptically.

"God's choice. Also the Bishop's." He could see I didn't care for prisons. "God is the friend of the prisoner," he offered, "when so many turn their backs on them."

I appreciated this and held out my hand. "Glad to meet you."

Getting to his feet, he introduced himself formally. "Father Thomas Moreno, the parish of St. Anne." There was authority in his handshake, as if he really had a vocation. We settled back in our respective places to gaze at each other, with everything to say but saying nothing.

Again he prompted, "This stuff on the beach, you said it never happened before?"

"No."

"Why do you think it happened?"

"Why? You mean 'how,' how the hell could it happen? Sorry," I apologized for the swear, but he wasn't bothered.

"If you filled me in," he said, "I could make some guesses."

As little trust in people as I had, I knew this might be my best chance. Besides, Rayna was also in danger. So I went at it obliquely.

"Did you ever see demonic possession?"

"You were possessed?"

"Not exactly."

At that point, Rayna jumped back on the couch and curled into her tight ball. I fussed with the bandage around her paw.

Apparently he wasn't infinitely patient. He leaned forward. "Lee, what happened this morning?"

"Well, what do you know about alien beings?" I murmured.

"Alien beings on the beach?"

"No, in general. Alien beings on earth."

He took this more seriously than I dared hope. "I haven't seen aliens on earth, but the universe is a surprising place. I did see what you'd call demonic possession in the mountains of Peru. But not here," making a little joke, "there's not enough passion here."

"I don't know about the demonic but I don't think I'm possessed," I answered. "Not now, anyway."

His gaze drifted to Rayna, studying her while she slept.

"She knows," he pronounced. "There was something real in the room with her, she wanted to bite it." He looked straight at me, black eyes alive. "Was she trying to kill what was on the beach?"

Of course she was! I thought, that was the hunter at the beach! My eyes darted away from his.

"You're afraid to talk about it?"

I shook my head evasively.

"Listen," he encouraged me, "it's better to talk about it."

I cleared my throat. "Talking about it makes me sound insane."

"And you're not?" he asked respectfully.

"Maybe, I don't know. If I am and I'm hospitalized, it would break Rayna's heart."

He gave that due consideration. "What if she was with someone you trusted?"

"If Rayna was all right?" I let myself picture the hospital, the daily meds, lying to the shrinks so they'd release me sooner. This time I shook my head with certainty. "I don't need a hospital, I'm not mentally ill. I'm just involved in something . . . complicated."

His expression invited me to go on.

"Can we keep this between us, just you and me?"

He nodded, but I stopped. If I speak this, I thought, it will change my life forever.

"My life will be different," I said.

"More than it's already different?"

I turned to the living room door and back to sleeping Rayna. I couldn't go back and I couldn't go forward. I felt something like despair.

He appeared to understand. "You suffered today."

"I could die, couldn't I?"

Surprised, he replied, "I don't know."

"Horror and pain," I explained.

"What do you mean?"

"Someone said there'd be horror and pain." I shut up quickly, but he picked right up on it.

"You, me, and someone else?"

"Well maybe that someone isn't real," I responded.

"Lots of people say God isn't real."

"I don't care about God."

"Yeah, but to me the most important things aren't real."

I said stiffly, "I know the difference between what's real and what's not," but that was exactly what I no longer knew. Trying again, I said, "I believe in things that can be proved, things you can measure. Solid things with substance."

Rayna chose this moment to stand up. I put an arm around her, the coarse black fur, the muscular body, a dog of substance. Gazing over at Tomás, I saw a very sincere man and knew we'd never agree about what was real and what wasn't.

"You're a priest, you're trained to believe the doctrine," I told him, intending to give an unbiased opinion. "But when I hear Christian doctrine, all I hear is mythology. The virgin birth, the resurrection of the body, holy communion, they're all myths. I'm sorry, it's what I think."

"That's all right, faith is a personal matter," he replied. Well, thank god he's liberal, I thought.

"But look," he went on, "you're in the middle of something extraordinary. You had flames on your back. You can't explain it, I don't try."

"I don't want the extraordinary. I want my life back, before . . . my life three months ago."

"What was three months ago?"

I knew he wanted to hear what had happened then, but I dodged. "I lived in a suburb of Boston. I painted watercolors, Rayna and I competed in agility. You know, where dogs run a course with obstacles. Rayna's very fast, it's a thrill to see her."

Tomás went along with me. "I'd like to. Is there agility up here?"

"I don't know, I never seriously looked," I confessed.

He walked through the door I'd just opened. "Why did you leave Boston?"

I shook my head slightly and stared him down.

"Were you attacked there?"

"I told you, it never happened before."

"What did happen today?"

I supposed I could say that much, and I knew it would help reduce the trauma.

"I was on the bluff, looking at the ocean, feeling the warm breeze, when the ground just disappeared beneath me. There was nothing under my feet, nothing but water below and air above. It hit me the Earth had vanished, and my heart—well my heart just broke. I couldn't see anything, so I stumbled down the rocks and fell on the sand."

He listened to me intently.

"Then the fire started. I was facing the sun and everywhere the sun touched, it began to burn. First it was my hands, then it was my face, then my back." I paused to breathe. "What did it look like to you?"

"It looked like you were fighting something, or trying to get something off you. I saw the flames when I got close."

"And you thought . . . ?"

He hesitated. "At first I thought it was a religious vision."

"A religious vision?"

"I'm sorry, it's just who I am. I don't mean to make it sound ok."

I remembered the way his eyes had shone at the beach, and wondered exactly who I was talking to. We sat at an impasse until he restarted the conversation.

"What about your family? Are they in Boston?"

"Rayna is my family," I answered with a bit of pride. "No, I do have kids, a daughter and a son. They're both married and living on the west coast." Feeling the relief of talking about family, I volunteered, "I'll see them at Christmas, both the families are coming here. Grandma at the winter beach is so picturesque."

Grandma at the beach with horror and pain.

Tomás had a similar thought. "Two months away," he remarked.

My pulse accelerated and I realized it was time I stepped up to my situation.

"Everything I say to you is privileged communication. Agreed?"

"Yes."

Settling deeper into the couch, with eyes fixed on the sunlight beyond the front window, I began.

"I left Boston because I decided it was too dangerous. There was—there is—a sort of voice in my head. It's not a crazy voice, it's extremely kind and good. I first heard it in August, and last September I dreamed a bunch of words and phrases about it. Like I was in danger in the city, and there were too many people down there to be safe. I was supposed to go find a winter beach and then I saw this little house on the web. My home in Somerville was rented just like that, and here we are. Rayna and I came up the beginning of October."

"What was the danger?"

I sighed with the heaviness of my story. "The voice says it's being hunted. It's hiding in my thoughts and somehow my thoughts protect it, or I protect it, I don't know exactly. The thing that's hunting it . . . ," tears began to run down my cheeks of their own accord, "that's what was on the beach."

Rayna stood up to sniff my face. "Get down," I whispered,

pushing her, and she hopped to the floor.

Tomás had been watching me gravely, but now he turned to Rayna again.

"She was fighting a mortal enemy, but it didn't hurt her and she wasn't afraid of it." He seemed to find this fascinating. "Maybe," he suggested, "it can't touch a dog's mind."

"She had to stay home today because she cut her paw yesterday," I explained. "The voice said I should always keep my spirit with me, but I didn't know he meant her."

"Of course she's your spirit," Tomás said, as if any fool could tell. "Don't be separated from her again. If you need anything, from town or anywhere, tell me and we'll get it for you."

"That's—," I was going to say "stupid," but realized he could be right. My life was shrinking before my eyes. "I prefer to shop for myself," I said.

"We have some wonderful ladies at the church who get things for our shut-ins. I think you'd qualify for that." I couldn't tell if there was a laugh behind his straight face. It certainly wasn't funny to me.

"Don't try to pass me off as a Catholic. And don't you have to let your Bishop know about me?"

"Pastor," he corrected. "I live at the rectory and I assist the pastor when I'm not at the prison. No, I don't think I need to tell him yet. You're not a danger to yourself or others. Are you?" He raised his eyebrows.

"Thanks a lot," I retorted and finally managed to laugh with him.

His cell phone chimed discreetly and he took his tea mug back to the kitchen. He'd bring my car tomorrow morning, he promised, and we'd talk more about the voice. Standing at the front door, he asked what I planned to do for the rest of the day. I was tempted to say, sit on the couch and stare into space, but told him I'd probably take a nap.

He wondered if his friend Janice could look in on me later. I didn't want any strangers looking in on me, but guessed he was thinking of my safety and agreed. Giving me his cell number, he urged me to text if I had any problems and not to let Rayna out of my sight. After he drove off, I realized he'd deliberately stranded me at home for the day.

It was barely ten in the morning and the day was still warm. I took Rayna out to walk around the house, tense with the possibility she might leap in the air, to tear an invisible enemy to pieces. But the lovely weather didn't lie and the cottage stood serene at the corner of its big side yard. A large and ancient apple tree grew in the center of the yard, leafless now and exposed in all its rough old age.

Rayna sniffed happily among the foundation bushes, as I let her take her time tracing rodent trails in the grass. When my legs hinted they couldn't keep me standing much longer, I looked around for the outside chairs. These were all in the basement where I'd stored them when the weather got cold, so I brought Rayna with me and cautiously opened the bulkhead doors. Nothing rushed us from the dark, and I let Rayna precede me down the stairs, into the delicious darkness where the mice hung out.

Carrying up two chairs, I set them under the eastern living room windows where I could sit in the sun and gaze at the apple tree. The lawn chairs were comfortable enough and I put my feet up on the second one, thinking how nice it would be to draw the apple tree in the snow. Today winter was far away, but would I even survive to see the snow?

The morning had messed me up in a bad way. No one had ever physically attacked me and it was shocking to be a victim of violence. Except there was no perpetrator, no physical evidence, and this strange guy healed me on the spot. The attack sounded like a fantasy, although he'd called it an illusion. But how would he know, they don't teach you stuff like that in divinity school. I only had his word he was a priest at St. Anne's, and I wondered if he'd actually return my car in the morning.

These thoughts lumbered around my brain, on this, the last beautiful day of fall. I made sure Rayna's leash was secure, rested my head against the back of my chair, and closed my eyes.

Rayna's barking woke me. It had become afternoon, we were in the shade of the house, and a little red car was slowing as it approached the cottage. Sitting outside with a barking dog was about as conspicuous as you can get, so there was nothing to do but wait until the driver came around the porch to greet me. She was a middle-aged woman with hair shorter than mine, and a purposeful stride.

"Hello," she called above the racket Rayna made, and I had Rayna lie down and be quiet.

"You met my friend Father Thomas, on the beach this morning," she said as she approached, confirming that she was indeed Janice.

Civility required me to indicate the empty chair beside me. She sat, extending her feet as though she'd been on them all day. Probably came right from work, I thought. Rayna stood on hind feet with front paws on the arm of her chair, staring into her face.

"Hello, dog," Janice said.

"Off," I commanded, and Rayna dropped back to the ground.

"I promised Father Thomas I'd just make a quick stop to meet you," she said.

"He was very helpful when I rolled down the bluff this morning," I replied.

"Yes, he's very capable. Lucky thing he was down there."

I asked cautiously, "Are you from the church?"

"Oh no, I'm quite secular," she answered.

"You know Father Thomas well?"

"Only since he came out from Chicago, and that was last June." She volunteered no more information, so clearly she wasn't one to gossip. Gazing into the yard, she remarked, "This is a pretty spot on a day like today."

"I thought I'd better enjoy it before the snow comes," I said.

"Oh, let's not rush that!" she laughed, and got to her feet again. If I could make jokes, I must be doing all right.

"I appreciate your coming by," I told her.

"Of course, any time," she replied graciously.

I watched her back her car out of the driveway and return the way she'd come. Well that wasn't too bad, I thought, friendly but not inquisitive. Also, she provided the valuable information that he really was a priest from Chicago and he was very capable.

The next day was a different day altogether. The weather was cold, my head was clear, and my thinking skeptical. I hadn't felt the voice's presence the night before, and suspected that that story had come to its natural end, a delusion that had run its course.

I was downstairs when Rayna barked to announce his arrival. He'd parked his car in front of the cottage and came to collect my car keys, before trotting off in the direction of the beach. About twenty minutes later my car was back in the driveway, and Rayna was greeting him enthusiastically when I let him in at the kitchen door. That was fast, I thought, they only met yesterday. But I was glad to see him too.

In the trap of my thoughts it'd been easy to doubt him, but here, alive and real at my kitchen table, Tomás inspired trust. He laid my keys on the table and gazed at me with open curiosity, as if I held an important secret.

"Thank you for bringing the car back," I told him.

"Tell me about the voice." He wasn't going to dance around. "What does it say to you now?"

"He isn't saying a darn thing." I could see Tomás adjust to my new, dismissive tone. "I think the illusion is done," I said. "There is no presence, probably never was."

"How about tea," he suggested. We didn't speak again until I set the mugs on the kitchen table.

"So the voice departed?" he asked.

"Well, I think so," I answered. "He used to make me feel peaceful when I went to sleep. To comfort me after I spent the whole day denying his existence. Last night there was nothing."

"Did the hunter leave too?"

"I suppose—," but I couldn't go on. Rayna was sitting beside me, and if I knew anything, I knew my dog. Tomás was right, the thing in the room had been real to her. "I don't know what it did." I got up. "Tomás, I don't want to have this conversation."

He nodded, keeping his seat.

"I don't want to know where the hunter is. I'm sorry I said yes to the voice."

"Tell me about it," he said, his counselor persona no doubt.

Resigned, I sat again. "I was doing yoga, floating in another space. I heard a voice asking if I would help it. I said yes, I don't know why. Then he told me there would be horror and pain, and he was so sorry.

I could feel his sorrow, it was very personal. I assumed he was talking about something mental, I didn't think it would be real, physical stuff."

"I don't know where the line is, between mental and physical," Tomás commented.

"Physical is where you could die," I said tartly.

"Yesterday was to hurt you, not kill you."

"How do you know?" I demanded.

He retreated. "You're right, I don't know. Was Rayna there when he asked for help?"

"Lying against my side."

"Did he pick you because of Rayna?"

"I don't think there was much picking, I think he just fell into my consciousness." I heard the words I said and quickly amended them. "I'm saying it's how it felt, I'm not saying it actually happened."

"It didn't?"

"I think I dreamed the whole voice thing. I want you to help me figure out why this stuff seems so real to me."

He considered me for a while, and I couldn't guess what he was thinking. Finally he said, "I can't do that. I spend too much time in the unbelievable."

"Just listen for any internal contradictions."

"Lee, I don't see why God put me in your way. It's my duty to seek out the poor, the afflicted, and the lonely, to strengthen them in God. The convicts, all they have is God, and it doesn't matter if they don't believe in Him, because I can pray for them. But what does your voice have to do with me?"

I watched him try to unravel this problem, gazing into the space in front of him until a flicker of excitement lit his eyes.

"It's why I was at the beach!" He flashed me a look of confidence. "That's how I had the power to heal you. My life—." He stopped himself and I knew, whatever it was, he guarded this secret carefully. With all that business about illusions and visions, he probably should.

Gazing at me with new interest, he asked, "Who is your voice hiding from?"

"The words were, 'it hunts me'."

"Hunts . . . ," Tomás pondered. "Why?"

"To destroy him."

"And destroy you too?" He frowned. "Can't you tell him he's got to go hide somewhere else?"

Without warning, I leapt to my feet, shouting, "No! Look how it hurt me, imagine what it will do to him!" Rayna stood, frozen and alert. I came to myself and a moment went by.

Sitting down, I said shyly, "I didn't know I cared what happened to him."

"Well, there you are," Tomás said softly.

"Where am I?"

"Your soul is committed."

"I don't know about soul," I muttered.

"Ok, then why do you care what happens to him?"

My silly eyes were tearing up. "I don't know. I'd say I loved him, if it wasn't so stupid."

"How is that stupid?"

"To feel love for an alien presence? It's ridiculous."

Shaking his head, he told me, "I believe in your love, and your alien."

"Tomás, I've been a crazy person for three months—."

"I've been a priest for fifteen years. I know devotion when I see it."

I wanted to deny all of it, but I had nothing to say.

He reached across the table to touch my hand. "You're on this road already. It's better if I come along."

Unsure of what I was agreeing to, I stared at our hands. Next to me, Rayna lay down on my feet, a warm and secure feeling.

"Tell me more about your alien," Tomás suggested.

Well, that can't hurt, I thought. "He's wise, he's a power for good."

"Where does he come from?"

I began to blush. This was so unreal I could barely articulate the words. "He . . . it was . . . is, he comes from another galaxy. In our world it's called NGC 300 and it's seven million light years away."

Tomás looked at me with the blank face of a sleeper. Then he blinked. "You're kidding, aren't you?"

Together, the three of us walked along the road, moving slowly to protect Rayna's paw. I was giving serious thought to the last two days, and had made up my mind that this was not how I wanted my life to go. The sensible decision was that nothing had actually happened, that I'd just tripped down a bluff and fallen on the sand. Tomás wouldn't be much help here because he claimed to believe in an alien, but maybe I could talk to his pastor.

"Tomás, listen, the more I think about it, the more I think I'm suffering from a delusional disorder. I've been very isolated since August."

He'd been pursuing his own thoughts and chose to ignore me. "Before I went to seminary," he said, gazing down the road, "I lived in Peru. I learned about good and bad energies, the benevolent and malevolent ones." He stopped to face me. "I believe in a vast and mysterious God."

Oh, I thought, that's how he could see the fire! For a moment it made perfect sense, then I got angry.

"You're so wrong, there's no mystery! I was a social worker. You hear how someone grew up, what happened to them when they were babies, and you know exactly what their life will be!" For some reason I was now furious. "I've been in a dream since August, I imagined the voice, I imagined the fire!" Then I remembered standing on empty air as the earth ended and my heart split, and there on the road I started to weep.

Tomás quietly took Rayna's leash from me. I stood and sobbed, close to hysteria but too proud to go there. After a few minutes of this, Rayna stood up on her hind legs and pawed my waist. I did what we always do after I've been away, I leaned over and put my arms around her, she nestled her muzzle behind my ear, and we stood like that, breathing together.

When I let her go, I was more or less ready to take on this preposterous life I'd wandered into. We walked back to the cottage, where Tomás got in his car to go to the rectory and become a priest. I was surprised by the pang I felt when his car turned the corner and disappeared. Then I roamed the cottage, the place where Rayna and I would be restricted until Christmas. Just eight weeks and my family would be here, and the story of the voice would be over. Because I was sure this craziness could not survive the normalcy of their visit.

My laptop was on the oak dining room table. I opened it, not clear what I wanted to do, and tentatively entered the search words "alien beings." The top hit was a list of supposed extraterrestrial creatures, each with a description and a charming sketch of its main characteristics. I was relieved that none of them had the least bit of interest to me. My alien, if I was willing to presume that much (and I wasn't), had no characteristics, except for a voice and the name of its galaxy. I'd never bothered about stars and galaxies, and I didn't know what an NGC was, but now was a good time to prove that none of this was real.

NGC 300 turned out to be very real, and a thing of astonishing beauty. It was a spiral galaxy, photographed in visible and ultraviolet light, with enhanced color, no less. I could scarcely take in all its magnificent detail. The yellow and blue pinpoints of stars, the spiral arms flung out in a soft, aqua-marine haze, its lemony-green center of older stars, and the delicate pink of heated gases and supernova, all against a background of the deepest black. I looked until I lost myself in disbelief, that this beauty could have anything to do with me. There was no way to explain the feeling I had, except to say that I belonged to this galaxy. This, obviously, was completely untrue.

Thanksgiving

Not only did Tomás return to see me, his visits became a regular thing. When Rayna's paw healed he drove us to the vet to get the bandage off. This wasn't really necessary because Rayna was beside me the whole time, but I think he wanted to keep an eye on us. We fell into walking Rayna together in the morning, and occasionally all of us went to the supermarket, where Rayna and I waited in the car while he shopped. We avoided talking about the voice or the day of the attack, acting as if we'd simply struck up an acquaintance on the beach one day.

The voice had completely ceased to contact me, neither in half-dreamt, late-night conversations, nor by helping me fall asleep. In some ways it was good not to be reminded of the voice, because the idea of an alien presence in my mind threatened everything I knew about the world. In college I loved the new field of neuropsychology, which mapped regions of the brain to human behavior. It perfectly fit my desire for a rational explanation of life, and allowed me to believe that a clear scientific process would always sort out the real from the unreal.

I found it touching, but naive, for Tomás to say he believed in the voice because I felt devotion to it. To my mind, devotion to an invisible presence was an article of faith, but I was grateful he believed me for whatever reason. So I stopped dwelling on my insanity and began to look for explanations of this strange experience I was having.

Aside from walks with Rayna and watching Netflix at night, I spent my time reading books or browsing the internet for information about the brain. A lot had happened in neuropsych, since I was in college and traumatic brain injury was the primary evidence of brain function. Now PET scans, CAT scans, and fMRIs could depict brain activity in detail. I wasn't looking for a complex explanation, just something that was a sufficient cause for what Tomás preferred to call the extraordinary.

Starting with the simplistic notion that something had entered my brain, it was obvious it would have to be extremely small. I read that nanoparticles were small enough to pass from our blood into the brain, and might even be used in the future to deliver drugs for some types of brain therapy. One study said the impact of nanoparticle movement through brain tissue had no bad effects and caused no disruption of neural circuits, which I found reassuring in case this had happened to me. Leaving aside the question of how the particles got into my brain, I considered a theory that the voice was a chain of nanoparticles that altered my thinking in some way. How nanoparticles enabled the voice to speak was way beyond the scope of my theory.

The days got darker and colder as November progressed, but Tomás never ducked our walks. He was from Chicago, he reminded me, so cold was nothing to him. Rayna's happy three-note bark always alerted me that he'd arrived at the cottage. When he came through the back door, she'd leap up in front of him like a spring toy. Then she'd twist around his legs until he squatted down and let her lick his face. If he was trying to endear himself to me, he'd found the right way to do it. I assumed he came to visit us because he missed ordinary family life, but it often felt like he came to reassure himself we were ok.

He wanted us to stay safe, which I understood, but his scrupulous caution produced annoying results. If I wanted library books, I'd have to request them through the online catalog and let him know when they came in. He'd make a trip to the library to bring them to me, and when I was finished, he'd make another trip to return them. The only time I could leave the cottage was on Rayna's walks, and I longed for a simple visit to the supermarket, where I could wander the aisles at will.

Weeks had gone by since the beach attack, with not a single sign of the hunter. Still, Tomás insisted on control. On one of our morning walks, I decided to complain.

"I don't know why you want to waste your time fetching books for me, but I have some more at the library. And you better not be telling the librarians I'm a shut-in, because some day I'm going to show up there, happy and healthy, and you'll be in trouble."

"You had a miraculous recovery."

"Oh, please," I said with distaste.

This hung in the air as we walked. Christmas would be here in five weeks and we were exactly where we'd been at the end of October.

"You know," I continued, "there hasn't been a word from the voice since the thing at the beach. Total silence, not even dreams. Do you think we made a mistake?"

"What kind of mistake?"

"There isn't any danger any more."

"No, it's the other way around. Silence means more danger."

"You're sure?" Actually, I missed the voice and wanted it to speak to me. "What do you think," I said, "could I ask him if he's still there?"

Tomás stopped so abruptly that ten feet ahead Rayna halted and turned to look at us.

"Ask the Voice? No! Do not ask him anything!" His black eyes gleamed with a hard light. Staring into them, I wondered what I'd just triggered.

He lowered his voice. "Malevolent spirits got here in October. They're still here, all around us, waiting for some crumb to drop." I would have interrupted but he was too agitated. "Do not, do not speak to the Voice. Not in your thoughts, never aloud!"

Who does he think he is, this kid from Chicago?

He read my resistance and deliberately turned his back on me. When he faced me again he was more himself. "Come on, Lee, they're not seven million light years away."

"Really?" I scoffed. "Rayna isn't worried."

Surveying the empty road where she stood waiting for us, he nodded. "No, she isn't," he agreed, and I took this as an apology. We began to walk again.

I pondered this man beside me, never married, no children, a guy who was clearly capable of love. How lonely had his life been? How lonely could it get?

"Why did you become a priest?"

"Both of my parents are undocumented. When I was little, *la migra*, the INS agents, they used to hang out in places where they could pick off people. Then they would deport them. One day my mom didn't come home from her cleaning job and I knew they'd grabbed her. I went a little wild, screaming at my sister when she told me to go to bed. My mom finally came home. She said she was waiting until the agents left the neighborhood.

"After that, I kept myself awake every night until my parents came home." He made a face. "My sister said I was crazy, and maybe I was. When I got to be ten I made a solemn promise to God, I'd serve him for the rest of my life if he kept my parents safe. After that it was easier, I let Jesus bring them home."

The poor little kid, I thought. What a waste of a good man. Impulsively, I reached over and laid a hand on his arm. "I'm so sorry—"

He caught my hand to push it off, then reconsidered and pressed it back on his arm.

"Ah, Lee, what you don't know," he reproached me. "There's no 'sorry' for me. I talked to Jesus when I was a little kid. I was always called to serve, I never had any doubts."

I would have withdrawn my hand out of embarrassment, but he wasn't giving it back.

We walked on a little ways and I said cautiously, "Are you happy with your choice?"

"God gives us sex and love to make us happy. But not for me, he gave me a different life."

He meant he was a person with a different design. Was he some kind of holy being, or just strange?

After a while he asked me, "Were you happy?"

"When I got married I was. I met Bill in college, he was captain of the running team. Very serious and thoughtful. He loved long silent runs and all his friends called him, 'Bill the Runner'. Back then, he was the most wonderful man I ever met." On this cold day in Maine, I remembered the bright light of our first married summer. "We married right after college, and both went to graduate school. Then we had our two great kids. It was exactly like it's supposed to happen."

But to be honest there was more to say, and I decided to say it. "I don't think anyone's ever happy for long. He was a solitary person, and after a while he turned into 'the Man of Few Words'. It was a family joke. When the kids grew up and left, it was only the two of us. With me he was 'Bill the Silent' and at the end there was nothing between us but the occasional touch." I could hear the regret in my voice.

By now I was quite comfortable with my hand imprisoned on Tomás' arm, as if we always walked like this.

————

Knowing I'd be alone on Thanksgiving, Tomás proposed we have a little Thanksgiving meal on Friday when he could come over. I was so ignorant, I didn't know if Latinos celebrated Thanksgiving, but I went online and learned that Latino Thanksgivings were a lot more fun than the Gringo version. The grandmas, mothers, and aunties all in the kitchen, bachata and merengue music playing in the living room all day, people drinking and dancing until dinner at nine o'clock. Then everyone squeezed on the couches and chairs, eating turkey, pork, rice and beans, sweet milk cakes, and flan.

Had Thanksgiving been that way for Tomás and his family, back in the 1970s? Did undocumented families mimic Anglos and sit down in their best clothes around a table with turkey, mashed potatoes, string beans, and pumpkin pie? Or did they congregate in the homes of their relatives to celebrate together? Or watch the Macy's Thanksgiving Day Parade and then go off to work. I didn't know.

My family drove out to visit the grandparents in the suburbs. While the men drank and watched football, Grandma cooked, the moms polished the silver and set the table, and the kids fooled around outside. In middle school I disdained watching football, but when I joined the women I lost my mind with boredom. Picturing gregarious Latino families full of life and music, I regretted the tedious Thanksgivings of my childhood. Bill and I did better with our kids, until he disengaged. After that we'd go to friends' houses for Thanksgiving.

There was no way I was going to create a sham Latino Thanksgiving for Tomás, with just the two of us. I cringed at the thought of Latin dancing with my friend the priest. But I did want to try cooking a flan. At first I thought we could make the flan together, until I realized that's what you did when you were falling in love—you took turns beating the eggs and milk and laughed over your mistakes. But we weren't two lovers discovering how to play together, or worse, a mother teaching a son how to cook flan. No, he'd have to instruct me, the Anglo, in how to make flan.

But between the parish and the prison, I was sure he wouldn't have the time, and he probably wasn't much of a cook anyway. I'd have to make it the day before and we'd see if it was anything like his mom's. I wanted to surprise him, but if he knew anything about flan, my shopping list of sweet milk, eggs, and vanilla would give the game away.

When it came down to it, he set the shopping bags down on my kitchen counter without comment. I supposed his posse of helpful ladies did the shopping.

Stowing the bags in the closet to unload after he left, I asked casually, "Did your mom ever make flan for Thanksgiving?" And felt instant regret, as I realized the answer had to be, "She worked two jobs, what do you think?"

"We always bought the flan," Tomás said pleasantly. "It was a big favorite."

The Friday after Thanksgiving he arrived late in the day, and we sat in the kitchen drinking beer. The squash was in the oven and the room was warm. He told me he grew up in an LA neighborhood with documented and undocumented families. His mom cleaned homes and offices and his dad did factory work, and when they weren't working they kept close to the house to avoid the INS. From when she was young, his older sister did all the translating at school and doctor's offices, even when she didn't understand what the grown ups were talking about.

It was a time when LA was changing from an almost all-white city to a city with lots of Latinos. Whites made noise that the Latinos were taking all the good jobs, and having babies so they could collect welfare benefits. INS agents would surround work places and deport anyone who looked Latino, even if they were citizens. It was a hard time to be Latino.

For Tomás, the happiest place was church. The parish priest was an Anglo who dedicated his life to helping the neighborhood families. Donations to the church, plus most of what the nuns raised, went to homes where a parent had been deported.

"You were fortunate," I remarked, "to have a priest like that."

"Yeah, I was. Our priest made a big impression on me, he was a true example of God's goodness."

I told Tomás about growing up in New York City, how my dad worked as a geologist for an oil company, but always managed to get us out of the city during the summer. It might be a mouse-ridden cottage, but it was always near the ocean.

"That's why I picked this cottage," I called to him, as he took glasses and silverware into the dining room. "It reminded me of those summers."

"You had to come here," he replied, standing at the kitchen door to make his point. "I was here."

"Is that right?" I advanced into the dining room with our plates, forcing him to step aside. "I don't have to do anything, not even for your friend God."

We laughed and sat down, but while we ate he looked at me curiously, the way he'd studied Rayna the day of the beach attack.

"So what?" I challenged him. "Do you think I was meant to come here? Do I have a mysterious purpose up here?" He shrugged and smiled and said he really liked how I cooked the squash.

I let it drop and got up to bring the flan. I'd never had Mexican flan before, but Tomás told me mine was as good as anything in LA. What a sweet guy, I thought, quite sure he was exaggerating.

We continued to sit around the table. "Janice told me you arrived last June," I said. "Why did they send you here?"

"I worked with Latino gangs in Chicago and the state prison here has a bunch of Latino guys. The Bishop wants me to bring God's grace to them."

"And what did you do to bring God's grace to the gangs?"

He smiled fondly. "We played a lot of soccer."

"All right," I replied with an edge, "but you don't play soccer in state prison."

"No, we don't," he said soberly. "No one is more afflicted than a convict. They're separated from everyone they love, they can't support their families, they do useless time filled up with card games and TV. COs insult them, bullies hurt them, steel doors slam behind them everywhere they go. Their kids grow up without them and their parents die without them. If God needs to be anywhere, it's with prisoners."

"You mean with a few of them."

"A person doesn't have to know God to be in His care."

"That's optimistic."

"It's what I can provide."

"Whatever you provide, they're still locked up. Doesn't it enrage the tiniest part of you that these guys are in prison?"

"It enrages you," he noted.

"Yes it does. When I was in first grade my parents sent me to the local public school because they believed in public schools. The first day of school the courtyard was packed, all Puerto Rican kids, poor, rowdy, no English. It was the kind of school where the teachers locked kids in the coat closet.

"I remember one day there was a little girl standing on top of her desk, sobbing, while the teacher ridiculed her. I don't know why she was on the desk, maybe she was dancing on it and the teacher suddenly came in the door. The little girl stood there with her hair hanging in her tears, not even raising her hands to wipe her face. It was horrible, she had no one to protect her.

"I was old enough to know the teacher was cruel. All year long I hated the teacher. Actually, I still hate that teacher."

"It could have been me, a generation later in a different city."

"But you would never dance on the desk. You were well behaved, weren't you?"

"In first grade I danced. I danced on desks until I made my promise to God. You don't jump around when you're serving God."

"Except when you're playing soccer."

"Yeah, except for soccer."

"I think I spent my entire life trying to fix what happened to that little girl."

"We're the same, you and me, we want to stop injustice in the world. I believe it's possible through God's love and you don't believe it can be done. But you try anyway."

"Maybe I'd be happier if I had your faith."

"I don't know if you want to be happier. You took on the burden of the poor and disadvantaged in first grade. It's a big job, but a worthy one."

I had to smile, he'd figured me out pretty well. For a while the conversation lapsed. Tomás appeared to have fallen into an internal debate.

"There's a kid," he began and stopped, turning his beer glass around in front of him.

"In prison?"

"Yeah, one of the convicts. They say 'cons'." He addressed the glass, maybe waiting for God's permission to speak. Or mine.

"I won't repeat anything," I assured him. He raised his head and gazed at me.

"This kid in prison, he sings. *Dios mío*, he can sing. When he sings, everyone around him goes quiet."

I heard what I thought was affection in Tomás' voice, and had to ask, "You like him?"

"Lee, he's my nephew's age. No, that's not what I need to talk about."

I hid my relief in a gulp of beer.

"God gave him a voice to sing for the world, he could be one of the great ones. Instead he goes with two friends to threaten a white kid with a baseball bat, because the kid owed money for drugs. Of course it got messed up, nobody knew what they were doing. There was a fight and the white kid died in the hospital.

"Darnell was sentenced to thirty and he's been in for five. In five years he learned to be a fighter and now he uses drugs he can't pay for, so he fights a lot. When he asks his mom for money, she cries on the phone because she doesn't have it and she knows he's going to get beat up. He tells me he used to be sweet and smart, he used to sing in church, and now he's a piece of shit.

"He won't talk about the murder except it was his fault, which is what he claims. If I say God forgives him, he tries to take a punch at me. I can't reach him, I can't absolve his sin or give him comfort. That's what I want to tell you, this kid breaks my heart."

I did my best not to fall into my familiar outrage. "Does—," I almost said "the Bishop" but realized Tomás would see it differently. "Does God want the prison to make you stronger?"

"I don't know what God wants. Right now it makes me doubt God's purpose. Too many guys, hidden and forgotten. I don't feel rage like you do, I feel sorrow."

"That's the difference between us," I said. "You're kind, compassionate, and noble. And I'm distrustful, stubborn, and angry. You bring as much of God as you can to the prison, but I sit in silence. I'm not doing anything for the little girl crying on her desk."

He shook his head. "No, you don't have any idea what you do. If I was God, I'd stay out of your way."

Hallucinations

The next day was the Saturday after Thanksgiving and I was restless, remembering how in previous years Rayna and I would have been happily tiring ourselves out at an agility trial. All morning I wandered around the cottage, bits of last night's talk snagging my attention and leading it down alleyways. I considered the little boy in LA who was afraid of the INS, and wondered how his older sister had done in life. She was the one I worried about, the one who had to take charge of the younger kids while the parents worked. She probably had her own kids now, and I should remember to ask Tomás about her.

I thought of the little girl in my first grade class, now probably an *abuela* with grandkids, maybe still living in New York or possibly back on the island. It occurred to me she might have done well in life, although in my experience it was just as likely she'd died in her twenties of a heroin overdose in East Harlem.

I wanted to get out of the cottage and move, and after lunch I decided to break the rules and try some hiking. There were supposed to be trails in the woods about five miles away, and although Tomás would almost certainly say no to the idea, Rayna and I couldn't stay cooped up until Christmas. The voice said to keep my spirit with me and I'd do exactly that. I got out Rayna's bright blue harness and my boots, and found my warm coat. Rayna had already jumped in the back of the car, when I realized the cold air was freezing my ears, and went back in the house to look for a hat.

During the move in October, I'd thrown a bunch of outdoor things into a large box that ended up in the little closet under the stairs. Pulling the box out and poking around in it, I found the blaze-orange knit cap I always wore in the fall. I took it out and stood with it in my hands, wondering what else I needed to bring. But my mind stalled, the thought slipped away, and I took the hat out to the car.

Parking at the trailhead, I clipped the tracking line to Rayna's hiking harness and we set out. The trail went down into the woods and I felt better right away, listening to the satisfying crunch of my boots walking through fallen leaves. The sun was out, the path was wide, and Rayna eagerly led out to the end of her line. We had about three hours until dark, an hour and a half out and the same back.

Cheered by a new trail to explore, I delighted in the lace work of the bare tree branches and the old arcs of berry brushes edging the path. I didn't pay attention to where we were because the trail was so clear, and instead I let my thoughts wander where they wanted. When I noticed the sun was working its way toward the trees, I stopped to check my cell phone. It told me the time was only one-thirty, and I marveled how different the angle of the sun was, this far north of Boston.

I went on at the end of Rayna's line, immersed in the pleasure of the hike, until I heard the shot. It wasn't close, but you don't have an outdoor dog in New England without knowing the sound: hunters.

Of course! It was the Saturday of Thanksgiving weekend, the last weekend of deer season, if I remembered correctly. This never mattered in the suburbs around Boston, but out here was a different story. Then I recalled what I'd left behind at the cottage—the blaze orange scarf I always tied around Rayna's neck during hunting season.

Suddenly anxious, I jerked the tracking line to bring Rayna close. Instead of coming to me, she erupted in outraged barking, throwing herself against the line and yanking me off balance. In a second, she had pulled me into the woods, my feet slamming down as fast as they could to keep me upright. I knew soon she'd be dragging me through the brush on my stomach, so when she dashed to the left of a big pine, I went to the right. The line snagged around the trunk and brought both of us up short.

She was in a frenzy, barking and lunging just like on the day of the beach attack. I tried to get a hand on her collar but she was never still, I shouted to her repeatedly but she refused to hear. Suddenly I felt a rush of intense rage and did something I couldn't account for: I reached out and unclipped the line from her hiking harness. She was swallowed by the woods in an instant.

It was dead silent. I gawked at the hand that held the empty harness clip, knowing that Rayna was streaking after whatever had infuriated her. She could cover ground like no other dog and it was hunting season. Weakly winding up the tracking line, I retreated back under the branches of the pine tree. What had possessed me to let her loose?

Then I saw that the sunlight was at the very tops of the trees. The sun was setting, but that couldn't be right, because it was one-thirty when I checked the time. I took out my phone and its face lit up: one-thirty. I pressed the home button, nothing, I tried to slide the screen, nothing. The phone was frozen on the last screen I'd looked at. With a flash of panic, I thought I was in a demonic forest where the sun, dogs, and phones, had all gone crazy.

An irregular burst of gunfire stuttered across the woods, like someone firing at a fast moving target. Silence, another ragged burst of fire, and it was quiet again. For a moment I listened for a yelp or a cry, then began to shout Rayna's name as loud as I could. When my voice gave out, I sat down on the pine needles, dusk settling around me, with no notion how this had happened. Rayna was gone, my phone was locked up, I was off the trail, and dark was coming quickly.

I'd never lost a dog permanently, although I knew someone who had. How long could you hope that they'd be found? And if they never came back, how could you not dwell on who might have taken them home, or if they died in the woods by bear, mountain lion, or bobcat? I kept myself calm. Kai had been known to run away and live in the wild for months, then one day walk back into their homes as if they'd never been gone. We were five miles out of town but I could post notices along the trail. The notices would say: "Do not chase her, she will run away! Put out food and let her come to you." I had to find out who managed this trail. Too bad we drove here, because Rayna hadn't learned the way home on foot.

At least there was no more hunting today, because now it was nearly dark. Should I try to find where I went off the trail and make my way back to the car?

Bad plan, because Rayna knew where she left me, so I had to

stay put. The cold was becoming a problem and I considered scraping together a pile of pine needles, digging a hole with my hands, and covering myself until dawn. No, that was lame, I wasn't a dog with a body temperature high enough to keep me warm.

I stood up to circle the tree and call again. Then I waited and listened, persuading myself to be patient, even though my mind was rehearsing tragic scenarios. It was dark when I heard a far off snap from deep in the woods. Something was moving out there and I had no dog to protect me. Peering anxiously into the blackness, I saw a faint point of light blinking on and off erratically. Watching it, I gradually concluded that someone moving through the underbrush with a flashlight might produce a light that looked like that.

When the hunter arrived, Rayna was hauling him after her by a rope tied to her harness. He was dressed all in camo, except for an orange hat identical to mine. My fingers shook as I tried to clip the line to Rayna's ecstatically twisting body, and the hunter had to hold her collar.

"That's a smart looking harness," the big man commented as he untied his rope from her harness. "Good color, that blue. I thought I heard a deer and this thing comes out of the woods like a rocket, starts chasing back and forth in front of me after something I couldn't see. I fired at it, I'm sorry about that, but the shots went high. Took me a bit before I could make out the blue. Don't know too many foxes wearing blue this year."

"How did you get her to come to you?" I asked.

"I tossed the gun and squatted down. Right away she stopped chasing and came over like we was friends." That didn't sound like Rayna but I didn't dispute it. This forest was way too spooky.

He had a phone that worked, and a buddy with an ATV that thundered down the trail to pick up Rayna and me. Sitting on the little back seat with my arms squashing Rayna to my chest, the ATV roaring and bouncing into the funnel of its headlights, I was happier than I'd been in months. Back in my car, I blasted the heat all the way to the cottage, while Rayna slept in her snug ball of fur, quite content with her adventure.

Once home and thoroughly warmed up, I looked at my phone to

see what its problem was. It displayed the correct time and otherwise appeared to be ok, which was not at all comforting. My mind started a slow downward spiral, trying to explain away each strange occurrence. Time had stood still, causing me to walk too far. One minute I held on to Rayna's line for dear life, the next I unclipped her. She ran in front of the hunter and he shot at her, then she came to him like a friend. And that intense rage, again.

I worked hard to convince myself that none of this meant anything. It was a hike that got weirdly exciting and might have ended badly, but came out all right in the end. In my confusion about the sound of shots and the setting sun, I forgot that the harness was bright blue, and now it was obvious there was never any serious danger to Rayna. Whatever lapse made me release her into the woods was probably caused by my frustration with her. And wasn't it great that we got to roar through the forest on an ATV?

As I buried my concerns about danger, my need to talk to the voice grew in proportion. Naturally, I wasn't going to say anything about this adventure to Tomás, but I knew Rayna and I wouldn't be going back to those woods for a long time.

———

I'd intended to begin a series of watercolors as soon as I was settled in at the cottage, and I'd left the paints out on the dining room sideboard to remind myself. But with only a month until my family arrived, I put the watercolors away, to clear the deck for what I thought of as my brain research. Being limited to internet articles, I didn't expect to find much more than a few mechanisms that would enable a voice to hide itself in my thoughts. Whatever the voice was (I'd stopped obsessing about its reality), I was determined it would be gone from my head by Christmas.

In college I wanted to know how people's brains worked, not their thoughts and feelings but the real stuff going on between their ears. After all, my father was a geologist and you can't get more concrete than rocks. Later I crossed over to clinical psychology, but kept one foot firmly planted in the verifiable domain of science. "Hiding in my thoughts" could be a metaphor, but I didn't think the voice used language that way. No, he had some type of substance and the place to look for him was in my brain.

I went online to refresh my knowledge of the cerebral cortex. There were six layers of neurons in the cerebral cortex and I was lucky to find pen and ink drawings of four different types of cells: the tiny pellet-shaped neurons at the top, below these the small triangular pyramidal neurons, then the large pyramidal neurons looking like witches hats with their long axons, and at the bottom the little multiform neurons that danced every which way. The drawings were delicate landscapes of the brain, graceful, detailed, and you could say whimsical.

Going back to the sideboard, I hauled open the big drawer of art supplies and took out my colored pencils. I could read all kinds of articles on the web, but think how much more productive it'd be if I also engaged my visual skills. Some intuition told me that my so-called research wasn't intended to discover an answer, but was intended to open a path for the voice to reveal the answer to me. So I sat at the dining room table and began to draw.

First, I drew an axon standing straight as a toothpick, a dome of dendrites branching from its top. This looked like a skinny tree with a crown of short leafless branches, so I drew more axons until there was a dense forest of axon trees climbing up the side of a steep mountain. In the next drawing, I made the tree trunks wider and drew little doors in them, from which, in tiny letters, came little cries for help. I tacked both drawings up in the hallway so I could ponder them during the day.

Later, I read about the interaction of neurotransmitters with specific receptors, and the effect of hallucinogenic drugs on this system. The fire on my skin could certainly have been a hallucination, and so possibly was the rage at the agility trial. I considered the day I heard the voice in the static, when I lay under a breeze from my open window, breathing deeply—a perfect setup for a paranoid fantasy about nanoparticles carrying drugs that would induce hallucinations in my brain.

Except of course it was hardly that simple. How did I arrive at a hallucinatory state three months later in October? Some absurdly long slow release drug? What about Tomás, was he hallucinating the flames he saw? And how about Rayna, did she hallucinate the thing she fought, assuming a dog could hallucinate? I checked online, and yes, dogs do behave oddly when they've eaten their owner's stash of acid, not that that proved anything.

Considering it another way, if I hallucinated fire on my body, I could certainly hallucinate Rayna's barking, and Tomás could be playing along for reasons of his own. But just as possible, older women could have health issues that affected their mental clarity, scheming priests could take advantage of them, and dogs could be frantic because they'd been left at home.

In the end, common sense asserted itself. No one was targeting me with hallucinogens for some unknown reason. It was also very unlikely that Tomás was a scheming priest, but it wouldn't hurt to rule out any health issues. I called a local clinic and embarrassed myself by asking if I could bring my dog with me to the appointment. They were very nice about it and I didn't have to resort to calling Rayna my comfort animal.

By day I poked around with half-baked neurological theories and by night I wished the voice would show himself again. It was a presence I cared about, a presence I . . . loved? Love was much too big a word. Tomás said he saw devotion and I supposed that was what I felt, but devotion didn't explain how badly I wanted him to talk to me. The longer he stayed silent, the more I had to hear from him. Slowly I became aware of an idea so tantalizing it became impossible to ignore. I didn't dare speak about it to Tomás because it sounded so grandiose. It went like this: What if I was destined to help the voice? What if I was the key to his freedom?

———

"Hi." It was Emily.

"Oh hi. How is everybody?"

"Good, we're doing great. I went away for a week on the project, and Phil did a good job with the girls. They think he's super dad right now. Did you get the email and all the Thanksgiving pictures?"

"It looked like fun, the whole family together."

"Except for you."

I ignored that. "Well, how did it go?"

"Not half bad. Phil came home early on Wednesday and took the girls to the pool and then out to eat. He got both of them to bed, which is no small thing with Cara, she thinks she can stay up as late as she wants. I spent the whole afternoon cooking, like, until one in the morning. It was great, nobody got in my way. I had the turkey and all the vegetables prepped and the next day David and Chris came early, so that helped a lot. Chris brought her strawberry cake and everybody pretty much behaved. The girls were even sweet to Davie."

"I bet it was great."

She hesitated a moment. "All of us decided, it's at David's next year."

"Oh, that will be nice for everyone!"

"No, I mean you too. You can get a direct flight, and they have a bedroom for you. Davie would love to see you."

I was silent.

"You can leave Rayna for just three or four days. You know she'll be all right."

"I need to find a good person to pet sit."

"You mean up there."

"If I'm still here."

"You haven't met too many locals? No nice retired guys?"

"Not really."

"Are you ok?"

"Oh I'm fine, I just had a full checkup. Apparently I'm doing great except for the back."

"I meant your mood. I thought I detected a note of resignation."

"It's dreary here, no snow, just cold." Suddenly I had an inspiration that would keep everyone far away from the beach. "You know, I can see if there's an inn where we could go! Big fireplaces, something much closer to Boston."

"Mom, that's stupid, it's way too late for that. The beach is fine, we'll go for long walks with Rayna. You do have the internet."

"Sweetie—"

"What?" she interrupted, catching the edge in my voice.

I lost my nerve. "You'll be surprised how deserted it is up here."

"Are you sorry you moved there?"

"I don't know yet."

"I wish we were coming sooner. You should make some friends. How bad can the people be, up there?"

"I have a friend. He's a priest and he works in the prison."

"Yuk, not a good prospect at all. You know, if I could change the tickets to something earlier, I'd do it, you know I would." She gave a sigh and changed the subject. "Are you watching anything on Netflix?"

"I spend my time pondering my destiny." We laughed at that.

———

There was an icy drizzle the next morning. Tomás and I walked with our shoulders up to our ears. He was unhappy there was no place to play soccer around here. At least in Chicago you could play indoors when the weather got awful.

"I talked to my daughter yesterday."

"Everything's ok?"

I stopped to face him so he'd pay attention. "No, not really. They'll be here in nearly two weeks. Isn't it time for divine intervention?"

"You mean from God?"

"Don't make fun of me."

"You want me to pray with you?"

I didn't know what I wanted from him, but it certainly wasn't a chance to pray. "You're the believer, you pray." He kept quiet and waited. "It's just a bunch of words to me," I insisted, "signifying nothing."

"You care about this . . . presence, he matters a lot to you. Your family matters. God will hear what you ask from the heart."

Had he been trying to convert me all along? "You're the one God pays attention to, so don't put this on me."

"What about your power? The Voice found you, not me."

"Look, I do research on the web, trying to figure a way out so my family doesn't walk into a mess. What do you do?" When he didn't reply, I added maliciously, "Do you suddenly think it's safe? Or do you plan to ask your buddy Jesus for help? Like on the beach."

I saw I'd actually annoyed him. We looked grimly at each other until I broke the deadlock by appealing to his training.

"I need your help. Can you please help me?"

He moved close enough for our shoulders to touch, murmuring, "It's too open to speak out here. We should find a church."

Careful not to roll my eyes, I pretended this was a reasonable suggestion. "Ok, I'll come with you."

We went to a neighboring parish, which meant we had to walk back to his car and drive in silence. I was full of misgivings. Not only was he controlling, he was becoming more paranoid. Leaving Rayna in the car, we scooted into the last pew of the church and kept our voices low.

Around us the walls were lined with white plastic statues, while small hanging ships swung their glowing red lights in the air currents. Tomás must have felt safer among the ships and plastic saints, because he faced me directly.

"I don't know how to help you. God can help, but you don't want that."

Truth was, I trusted myself more than God. "I feel like I have to do something," I said.

"Like what?"

"Take some action, find out what the situation is. I don't know if the thing hunting the voice is still around. I don't even know if there's a voice anymore."

"I'm sure there is."

"Then I'll talk to him."

Tomás averted his eyes, just for a moment, but I felt an emptiness opening between us.

"Don't you see how dangerous it is?" he asked.

"If it's dangerous for me, it's dangerous for my family. The voice will know what to do."

"Is this your power or your stupidity?"

"How about you do the praying and I'll do the asking?"

He gazed at something behind me, probably the one he thought was his savior. When his dark eyes came back to me, I saw how troubled he was.

Ignorance

I didn't sleep well that night and was glad when Tomás failed to show up the next morning. After I brought Rayna back from her walk, I sat in the kitchen trying to work out what had happened between Tomás and me. He acted like my turning to God would make the difference, but surely God wasn't waiting to hear from me after a lifetime of silence.

It had seemed so promising, when Tomás put his hand on my back and cold cascaded over me. I thought he had a special gift for healing and would return me to the sensible life most people lived. Instead we only waded in deeper, until now he'd called me stupid. He was a nice man, perceptive and kind, but crazy in some fundamental way (probably scarred by years of trying to keep his parents safe). And he was totally wrong about my power, I was helpless in my ignorance about the voice.

I got up and circled through the hallway, ending up back at the kitchen table. What physical evidence verified the existence of the voice? Nothing, not even Rayna's leaping and barking on the day of the beach attack. Maybe that was something silly, like a wasp that had revived in the heat of the furnace, and refused to die.

But the evidence of my experience was more complete. I wrote it down chronologically:

1. August: I heard or dreamt a voice when I did yoga. I experienced unexplained rage at an agility trial. I dreamt words that told me a presence in my mind was hiding from a hunter.
2. September: I had a nightmare and understood my rage came from the hunter. I found this house the same night and rented it in a week.
3. October: I moved to this house and heard a voice speak directly to me. A few weeks later I left Rayna at home and experienced

an illusory attack on the beach. When I got home Rayna was fighting something illusory in the house.

4. November: I took Rayna on a new trail, my cell phone stopped, Rayna barked at something illusory and ran away. A hunter almost shot her but she came to him. My cell worked when I got home.

What struck me immediately was how much my life had been disrupted. That, and how often I used the word "illusory." It was as if something had intervened to remove me from agility, drawing and painting, my kids and grandkids, and even my home in Somerville. Illusions had taken over, seemingly out of nowhere and for no purpose. I was quite sure none of this had been caused by me or my past, and pretty sure I hadn't unconsciously desired it.

Or had I? Why had I pretended to explore unknown places beyond my consciousness? I was never that type of person. Yet I'd been floating in an open and generous space, and the suspicious part of my nature must have been asleep. The voice in the static had asked for my help and I agreed—how easily I accepted him and upended my life. Did he sense danger now and hide himself, or did he slip away to save Rayna and me from harm?

Or was he waiting for me to save him? As if protecting my family wasn't enough.

I went back to the laptop where I'd been looking at functional MRIs, images my father the geologist would have loved for their ability to show actual brain activity. He was a hard man to please, and I never knew if he regretted that I switched from neuropsych to clinical practice. For that matter, had I gotten what I wanted from clinical practice? Had I repaired the injustice of little girls made to stand weeping on their desks? No, I didn't think so, not yet.

I wasn't getting what I wanted from my so-called brain research either. I'd been looking at various functional areas of the brain, wondering if the voice hid himself in different areas to escape detection. But I was weary of these theories wrung out of ignorance, and often ended up drawing rather than reading. So far, nothing had stepped out of the shadows of brain neurology and tapped me on the shoulder to say, "Here, you'll find your voice here."

Now I made two lateral views of the cerebral cortex, labeling the functional areas and adding a mass of new neural paths between them, to give the voice more places to hide. With shameless magical thinking, I colored the speech production areas blue to represent the voice (it seemed like his color), and connected these areas to the amygdala, in the hope it would prompt the voice to speak to me. He must know I wanted to hear from him, but he remained silent.

Becoming fanciful, I drew magnified views of the cerebral cortex, creating little towns in the valleys between the cortical ridges, with little voice people going about their business. I hung the new drawings in the hallway beside the earlier drawings, feeling the increasing pressure of time.

———

The downstairs was bright, as afternoon sunlight flooded the dining room windows. I lay down on the living room couch and pulled the blanket up under my arms. I'm not doing this alone, I thought, I'll stay safe like Tomás wants. Patting the blanket, I invited Rayna to lie on top of me. She cautiously stepped up on the coach and settled herself on my stomach, pleased with the body contact. I'll try this only once, I promised myself.

The night before I had developed my question, in simple words and present tense, and I spoke it aloud to the living room.

"When are you free?" Baby talk for a being that could travel across light years.

I began to repeat the question in my mind, matching my breath to the phrase until the words filled the space around me and I fell sleep. I woke when Rayna dug her paws into my stomach and jumped to the floor.

Sitting up, I had to get my bearings, because the dream had been remarkably vivid. A wolf was tracking a trail of blood through a hemlock forest. Her nose skimmed the hard packed snow searching for drops of blood, and at times she raised her head to scent the air and change direction. She trotted past huge standing trees, and pushed through the snow under fallen logs when the trail led that way. Coming into a clearing under blue sky, where the delicate tops of hemlock seedlings cast spiky shadows on the sunlit snow, she crossed back into the forest with its shadowless, milky light. In the dream it was certain that she would track her prey, corner it, and tear it to shreds.

My reaction to this dream was disappointment. If I was going to help the voice, I needed instructions, not allegory. The wolf was large and grey, and I didn't think she represented Rayna. Browsing online for wolf symbolism, I came up with three useless choices: a source of sacred wisdom; something threatening, evil or sly; and taking control of one's life. It did occur to me that the wolf might represent me, but that felt totally wrong. I hated hunting and killing, and Rayna was the hunter in the family. Didn't the voice know who I was by now?

When Tomás texted he could walk the next morning, I wanted to tell him to stay away. Against his orders I'd risked speaking to the voice, and failed to produce anything useful. Not only was it a failure, but it meant I'd have to talk to the voice again, sinning not once but twice. Still, the dream was a communication from the voice and I needed to hear his opinion of it.

When he entered the kitchen the next day, he looked somber and spent longer enduring Rayna's kisses, as if there was solace in them. He's holding our last conversation against me, I thought, feeling a thread of anger rise to the surface. As we started walking, I let the tracking line play out so Rayna could forge ahead. Tomás caught the line, drew it in and pushed it back in my hand.

"Be safe, Lee," he told me.

"Oh right," I mocked, "it's a long thirty feet." Then I lied, "I am being safe."

With this bad beginning, we set out.

After an extended silence, he asked, "Do you remember Darnell?"

"The one who sings?" At the moment I didn't give a damn about Darnell.

"He's in solitary for two weeks. He got jumped by some guys and put one of them in the hospital. It's his second offense, the next time he's going to get six months."

So it wasn't me Tomás was upset about. "Six months of solitary?"

"Twenty-three hours in the cell, and one hour out to take a

shower. For some guys they bring the shower into the cell."

"And what does six months in isolation do to a kid?" I demanded. "How are you supposed to bring compassion there? I'd burn the place down."

"You might," he muttered.

"How do you stand it?" It sounded like I was accusing him, although I didn't intend to.

He stopped and turned a desolate face to me.

"What's hard to stand is the cruelty, convicts on convicts, COs on convicts. Most COs are trained, but there's a few . . . they think they should make the place a Hell to punish the guys for their crimes. They forget the punishment is being locked up."

He wants my help, I realized, but I had no help to give him. I felt only anger, and deliberately looked away into the woods. The prison system was unjust, it wasn't going to get fixed, and his God wasn't doing a damn thing about it. Then I thought I saw an opportunity to spread enlightenment.

Turning back to him, I said, "Why don't you take God out of the equation?"

He stared at me.

"Stop torturing yourself about God. God is no help." This, I felt, was my chance to shine the light of reason into the dark of belief. "Waiting for God to be merciful is a waste of time. Humans created the mess, humans will fix it."

From his expression I realized I ought to be more positive. "We all have personal strength. You have lots of personal strength, if you just look," I said, but this had no effect.

There'd been too many days of isolation, too many days of fear, and besides, I'd lied to him. Now I was on a tear. He wasn't listening to me and never would. He'd always discounted me, never paid real attention to me. It must be automatic to him, a man who believed he represented the son of God. It's a good thing priests never married, I thought, their marriages wouldn't survive.

I took a stab at a place he might be vulnerable. "You've always been protected by the church. I don't think you know how real people live."

He glanced at me with surprise, and I felt a tingle of satisfaction. "I'm sure when you speak to your parish people, they agree with you because they're nice. You may think you know your prisoners, but really you don't know shit about them. You live in a fantasy of God's mercy and goodness."

He raised a hand in protest, but didn't speak.

"You don't value anything I say. I told you I was doing brain research, I do know something about neuroscience, and I'm trying to get the voice free. Your God and your faith are gumming up the works—."

Here Tomás interrupted. "You think you can save the Voice by knowing?"

"That's normally how people solve problems," I replied acidly.

He crossed his arms, implying he had all day. I thought, that's what it looks like when a nice priest gets angry.

But I'd burned all the bridges and was enjoying the fire. "I made some progress. More than you have, with your useless paranoia about evil spirits." Silence from Tomás, so I took my chance. "I had a communication from the voice. In a dream, he talked to me." Grabbing at words, I tried not to betray myself. "I mean the voice spoke to me through a dream. It was him, I know it."

I had Tomás' attention, if not his good will.

"I dreamt a big wolf was tracking something through the woods. It was totally silent except for her paws clacking on the crust of snow. There's only a drop of blood here and there, but she moves along like she's being led by the scent, running around trees and jumping over logs. The dream didn't actually end, but there wasn't any doubt she was going to catch the prey and kill it."

With a guarded look, he asked, "Rayna?"

I shook my head.

"You?"

"Oh, I don't know," I said, as if it didn't matter. "What do you think the wolf is doing?"

"She's hunting something."

I was about to ridicule this brainless answer, when I looked at his black eyes and hair, so right with his skin color, and felt a rush of longing. And quickly extinguished it.

"Well, obviously," I said coldly. "But what does it mean?"

"It means you're going to do whatever has to be done."

"But that doesn't tell me anything!" We're having a fight, I realized.

"It tells me everything."

"Oh, you're such a jerk!"

"Let's go." He took Rayna's line out of my hand and started back to the cottage. She looked at me to be sure I was following.

Watching his solitary form walk away with my dog, I regretted everything I said. Where had my spite come from? The poor man was only following the faith he learned, doing what he was taught to do. I hurried after the two of them and gave his arm what I hoped was a reassuring squeeze. When he ignored this, I did indeed feel stupid. As far as he was concerned he had Jesus and God backing him up.

———

We walked home in impenetrable silence, and I could barely bring myself to nod good-bye when he got in his car. I wanted nothing more to do with him that day, or possibly forever. It was a relief when I could shut the kitchen door, sit down, and sink into the muck of my anger, guilt, and regret. Rayna sat by my knees and I ran my hand down her back, over and over from ears to tail, hoping to find some comfort.

Why did I have to be so destructive? I never fought with Bill because it was pointless to yell into his silence, and now I was trashing a guy who wasn't even family. Probably I resented his dominance more than I realized. Still, I had achieved a result, because I'd gotten him to back off. It might be the ruin of our friendship, but at least now I had the freedom to do what I wanted, whatever that was.

It was less than two weeks until the family arrived for Christmas, a short time to wrap this up and get the voice safely back at NGC 300. On the other hand, it took only three minutes after the Big Bang to create fusion in the universe, so what was I worried about? I wanted a road map for freeing the voice, but no one was providing any, except possibly for the useless dream. Only I was no wolf, and had no teeth to tear the hunter apart.

With opportunity dwindling, I decided to commit myself to a

bold action. I could write questions to the voice on post-it notes. I didn't know if this would pass the test of not speaking to the voice, but I was willing to risk it. Who are you? I wrote. Is it safe to talk to you? How can I help you? I stuck the notes up around the cottage, but took them down the next day for fear Tomás would see them. That is, if he ever came to the cottage again. Besides, they had produced no effect overnight.

Tomás didn't show up the whole week. Several times I considered texting him with an apology, but I was stopped by shame about my disobedience and the insults I'd heaped on him. Advent was a busy time for priests, I told myself, and anyway, Tomás wouldn't want to know what I was doing.

I walked Rayna in the mornings and in the afternoons read about the brain. The question that troubled me most was whether the voice had left and taken the danger with him (leaving me to resume the life I'd once had), or if he and the danger remained with me. So I decided to conduct a simple experiment to test which was the case. Putting Rayna in the back of the car, I drove west out of town, then went north and east until we intersected the shore road five miles up the coast. This, I thought, would conceal where we were going from Rayna. Turning south on the shore road, we passed frozen marshes, and assorted motels and restaurants closed up tight for the season. I was dimly aware that what I was doing was either daringly bold or incredibly dumb.

It was a cold, sunless day and the shore road was empty. Approaching from the north I slowed as I saw the high bushes surrounding the beach road, and eased into the left turn. Without warning, Rayna sailed over the back of the front seat and landed in my lap, blocking my view of the windshield.

"Crazy dog! Get back!" I yelled, jerking the wheel hard to the right, my sight filled with Rayna's black face.

The left front of the car dipped into gravel, rose out of it, and we headed straight across the shore road toward the marshes on the other side. I yanked the car back to the left, swerving into the oncoming lane with no idea of what might be coming toward us. Rayna twisted in the narrow space of my lap, stepped onto the passenger seat, and sat down, where she gazed out the front window like an elegant tourist dressed in black. Beyond the windshield, there was no oncoming traffic as far as the eye could see.

Steering us back to the right-hand lane, I pulled into the first parking lot I found.

"You think I'm an idiot, don't you?" I asked her. She stared back at me with her dark, mysterious eyes.

Back in the safety of the cottage, I stood in front of the drawings in the hallway. Their whimsey was deceptive, as they concealed the possibility of horror and pain. I gave Rayna credit for being wiser than me when it came to unseen threats, and she'd had no doubts about the threat waiting out on the beach. I had to believe that danger and the voice had stayed behind, which promised a dreadful Christmas. I had to make the voice talk to me.

Post-its of written words were too crude, but as I looked at the drawings, another way occurred to me. What if I embedded questions for the voice in my drawings? The questions would have to be so well hidden that only someone who knew me intimately (had been part of my mind for months, for instance) could see them. Instead of speaking the questions aloud, I could simply hang the drawings in the cottage, and run a question through my mind every time I passed one.

I chose various functional areas in the brain that offered enough size and complexity to embed my questions, and began the drawings. It was tedious to hide words in lines and tones in such a way that the letters were obscured, and I became engrossed in the visual puzzles I had to solve. When I was satisfied a question was unreadable, I added the drawing to the gallery of neurological fantasies in the hall. That night, I went to bed with an excited feeling of accomplishment.

It was the next day that I made my discovery. While browsing, I happened to come across an online paper about the role of brain waves in enabling communication between regions of the brain. It was the first study I'd come across describing how areas of the brain communicated, and I read the paper avidly.

There are five types of brain waves, and each type is associated with a different level of mental activity, from the slow waves of deep sleep to the fast waves of cognitive high performance. According to the paper, each type of brain wave has an excitable phase and a non-excitable phase. Communication between regions can occur only when the excitable phase of the sending neurons is synchronized with the excitable phase of the receiving neurons.

That made sense, but what really got my attention was how important this wave synchronization was to thinking. Synchronization serves as a frame of reference for the information carried by the cognitive high performance waves, so that wave synchronization becomes the basis for human cognition. I held my breath at the audacity of describing how thinking happens, and then I understood that this was where I would find the voice.

I searched eagerly for more papers on brain waves and immediately discovered an article on nested oscillation. Nested oscillation is where the maximum height of a smaller, faster wave, like gamma, is coupled to the excitable phase of a taller, slower wave, like alpha. The paper said it had been proposed that this coupling underlies the discrete nature of perception.

Here I had to lift my head and gaze out the dining room windows to the dark spruce trees beyond the driveway. That's how it works, I thought, it's wave energy!

The voice was wave energy. This resolved so many problems, like how he fit into my brain. The voice's energy suited my brain perfectly, because it was like my own brain's energy. As for how he hid, he must be a master at things like nesting and synchronization. Of course it was crazy complicated, something we wouldn't be able to understand for decades. It suddenly touched me that this energy, so similar to my brain's energy, had been part of my mind since August.

Filled with new ideas, I shut the laptop and roamed around the dining room. If perception occurred through the coupling of a smaller, faster wave with a bigger, slower wave, that changed my understanding of reality. I used to think that vision, hearing, and touch brought the facts of the real world into our minds, where we could think about them. But no, now I could see that it was the wave energy in our brains that created the world we perceived. Nothing was real, except the energy of our thoughts.

I couldn't say if this radical shift in perspective was something the voice suggested to me, or if I was simply ready to let the concrete world go, but my new understanding was exhilarating.

I wandered into the kitchen, free of worry, and thinking it would be a great day to make soup. Getting out a pot and the chopping knife, I assembled onions, garlic, and carrots, and began to chop them. I didn't know yet how my new understanding of perception and reality could free the voice, but I was confident I'd discover that soon. Today it was enough to know that our brains created our experience, reality was fluid, and the voice's energy mixed with mine.

"Damn!" I cursed, and raised my hand. Blood was welling from a finger, so I stuck it under the faucet to stop the bleeding. In the bathroom I found a bandage and wrapped it tightly around the cut. But back in the kitchen, I looked around me with no idea of what I'd been doing. My mind was blank. Why was I even making soup, when I had so little time to set the voice free? I went to the dining room and opened the computer to the article about gamma waves nesting inside alpha waves, and tried to understand what it said. It made no sense to me and I closed the web page, because it had nothing to do with the voice.

The sun was setting and I could feel the draft from the windows. I should have rented a nice cape overlooking the water, I thought, and next year I would. Rayna was asleep on the couch, so I sat beside her. My family would arrive in six days, danger lurked at the beach, and Tomás was absent. Swept by a feeling of panic, I remembered how I wouldn't help him, and now I couldn't help the voice. What would it feel like if the voice was destroyed? Was that the pain and horror the voice had warned me of? For him, for me, or for my family too?

Desperation was eroding my sense of judgment. It didn't seem good enough to let the questions hang mutely on the wall. I stood up, unintentionally waking Rayna, and went to the hallway where the unanswered questions were on display. Rayna followed with curiosity.

Gazing at the drawings, I made up my mind. Laying the palm of my hand on the first hidden question, I bent my head to the paper and spoke it.

Nothing terrible happened. My words vanished into the quiet of the house, and I felt slightly reassured. I put my palm over the next drawing and waited for a long minute, until it seemed I'd better get this done. After speaking the second question, I moved from drawing to drawing, saying the words and becoming braver with each question.

I went to bed, optimistic that the voice would help me make a plan, and dreamt confused dreams of nested brain waves. The next morning I woke up with a headache.

———

It was eight days before Christmas, and the weather was finally predicting snow. The morning was still sunny and I wanted to get Rayna walked in case the storm came early. I was slipping her collar on, when we heard a car in the driveway and she raised her welcoming series of barks. I considered hiding upstairs before Tomás saw me, but my head hurt and he was already out of the car.

I opened the kitchen door with a stiff smile. Neither of us said a word as he and Rayna went through their ritual greeting, and as we walked down the kitchen steps. There was a lot to be said, but the cold pinched my nostrils and made my head throb.

Rayna was eager for a walk, so I gave her leash to Tomás and hung back to nurse my headache. The two of them drifted further and further ahead, until he glanced around and stopped to wait for me. This was the guy I'd insulted, lied to, and refused to help.

"What's up?" he called as I got closer.

I supposed this head pain was my punishment for being a lousy human being. "Just a headache. Go ahead with Rayna."

Instead he waited for me, and when we stood together, got right to the point. "I kept away all week, trying to understand you."

I wasn't in any shape to discuss this. "It's all right if you want to walk her by yourself. I'll go back."

"I'm sorry I made you angry. I'm sorry I didn't give you the support you needed."

Wordless before this generosity, I stared at the ground.

"I prayed to understand who you were. I didn't know, I couldn't see it." I wondered where this was going. "Sometimes I'm blind, but the Lord finally got through to me."

I nodded carefully because my head hurt.

"The Lord told me to trust you. You were chosen to lead, and I can serve. I'll help you however I can."

Headache

We walked back to the cottage, but I wasn't up to talking. My heart ached at how good he was, and my head ached just because it ached. When he left, Tomás peered at me and told me to let him know how I was doing in the afternoon.

By afternoon I couldn't concentrate on anything. The headache worried me because I never had headaches and the pain kept increasing. Also, I was afraid that Tomás had been right all along, and I was now in more trouble than I could imagine.

I stood up from the computer and a shock of pain knocked me back to my chair. Laying my head on the table, I heard Rayna growl in her throat. With a racing pulse, I straightened up as slowly as I could, until I was able to turn around. Rayna crouched ten feet away, slit eyes fixed on me, the fur raised between her shoulders. I was pretty sure there was nothing in the room with us.

"Rayna," I whispered, "What's wrong?"

She backed further away, her lip rising over a canine tooth. I was the problem.

I made my way to the kitchen and took naproxen, and still the headache deepened. By now the skies were lead-gray with approaching snow. I went slowly through the cottage checking that the windows were locked tight, while Rayna trailed me, ears flat, tail bent down, a canine accusation. When I called her she didn't come, when I looked toward her she backed off. If I had any doubts about the stupidity of speaking to the voice, they vanished before the distress of my abandoned dog.

It got dark early, the wind picked up, and by six it was obvious my mind was under siege. I had a hard time making out the letters on my phone, but I managed to text Tomás that my head was worse and I needed him. Squinting to make out his reply, I read he'd be there as soon as he could.

When he arrived I was lying on the living room couch, holding a cold pack to my head. He had paused in the dining room to remove his clerical collar, when Rayna rushed out from the corner she defended, whining and crying around his feet. Kneeling on one knee beside her, he promised her we'd get through this.

He brought a dining room chair up to the couch and sat down, his expression guarded.

I whispered, "I'm an idiot."

"Maybe," he said, taking the cold pack from me.

Placing his hands above my ears, he closed his eyes and bent his head, no longer interested in me. It was dead still. I let my eyes close, and after a while the pain softened somewhat. I felt a slow pulse across my forehead, and prickling where his fingers touched my scalp. Neither of us moved, but as small tremors shook his hands, I didn't dare open my eyes. The force of his concentration was beginning to frighten me . . .

Something inside my head popped, Rayna barked once, and Tomás crashed to the floor.

A brief gap in time, then deafening barks split my ear. I managed to turn my head and make out Tomás lying on the floor, face down, with Rayna jumping on his back. In the midst of the din she caused, I heard him wheeze. Now he rolled onto his side, arms over his head to protect himself from the wild animal. I got hold of her collar and hauled her against the couch. Free of the jumping dog, he began to cough.

I made Rayna sit until the fog in my brain lifted. When she was quiet, I slid to the floor to help Tomás sit up against the couch. He had the gray lips of someone who's kissed death, but then he groaned and took a labored breath. I felt a wave of relief.

All of a sudden he was on his feet, shouting with deranged fury in a language I'd never heard before. He cursed each of the four directions, the ceiling, and the floor, hurling his wrath into every corner of the room. Stopping as suddenly as he began, he stood at the center of the rug as if disoriented. Rayna and I didn't move, it seemed way too dangerous.

Eventually he touched his chest gingerly. "Oh Christ," he whispered and I thought he might break down. Seconds passed as he pulled himself together and his expression hardened. When he took a step toward the couch, I scrambled to get out of his way. Giving me a hostile look, he went and sat at the other end of the couch, staring straight before him and unconsciously clenching and unclenching his fists.

Rayna approached him silently, but he ignored her and she came back to me.

Speaking softly, I said, "You got rid of it."

"Curses I learned in Peru. Useless."

"But look at Rayna," I prompted. She was leaning against my legs in complete trust.

He turned a frozen face to me, and I thought I saw fear hiding in his eyes.

Softly again, I asked him, "What was it?"

"It—," he looked away to locate the right words. "It's not human."

My stomach tightened. I wanted to ask if we were in over our heads, but when I spoke what I said was entirely different. "I'm sorry you got hurt."

That seemed to make him angry.

"No, I am," I insisted, because this was important. "You have to be careful. I don't want you to die."

This silenced both of us, and we looked at each other, absorbed in the moment. Then he reached down the length of the couch and squeezed my fingers, harder than I expected.

He started coughing again, and had to stand to ease his chest. Seeing him on his feet, flexing his shoulders, I remembered he was a soccer player, and no doubt equal to all kinds of physical shock.

––––––––

We went into the kitchen where it felt safer, and sat side by side, like two survivors of a serious accident.

"How are you doing?" I asked him.

"Heart still works," he replied, laying a hand over his sternum. "It's going to hurt worse tomorrow."

"Can I . . . do you want . . . ?" I started to get up, but he touched my sleeve and I sat down.

"All my life," he began, "my whole life, I had to save people. It was *papi* and *mamá* when I was a kid, then it was my seminary brothers, and in Chicago it was the kids in the gangs. I save everyone, it's why God put me on earth." He glanced at me. "But I can't save you."

"You saved me on the beach and tonight you saved me."

He seemed about to argue, but fell into silence instead.

I lowered my voice, not knowing if it was ok to ask. "What was in my head, exactly? Could you feel it?"

"Yeah, I felt it, it didn't hide. It was all rage and fear. What it wants is destruction, and it fears . . . just about everything. It's powerful but it thinks it's all-powerful, and it hates goodness. That's as far as I got before it hit me."

"Why did it shock you?"

"I made it angry. I wanted to move it out of your mind, so I pushed it in different ways, looking for a weak place. I didn't find any."

"And you couldn't sense the danger?"

"I completely missed that."

Then I asked the obvious question. "Is it the thing that's hunting the voice?"

He nodded, and shrugged regretfully.

A strange question occurred to me. "Do you think . . . ?" I hesitated, " . . . does God have jurisdiction over this thing?"

Shooting me a look, "You don't believe in God."

"That's why I'm asking you."

"You mean, is God also the God of aliens?" He pondered this and I understood we were in deep waters. It took him a while to sort it out.

"We teach that God contains everything that is. He's the Creator and Ruler of the universe. Even the benevolent and malevolent spirits, they're part of God's great universe.

"I never made a difference between divine mystery and ordinary life, because I had visions all the time. Sometimes when I consecrate the Eucharist there are drops of blood on my hands, not drops of juice, real blood. Once—I don't tell people this—I washed Christ's feet at noon. The cobblestones were burning hot in the sun. If people knew I felt this heat, they'd say I was too devout, or a little cracked. But they'd understand it was part of the human world.

"Your Headache is nothing like that." His hand went back to his chest, as if to soothe remembered pain. "I believe this actually happened and tomorrow I'll have bruises to prove it. But it's beyond my faith. I know the God who belongs to this world. The Headache is not part of that."

The windows rattled with a gust of wind, making the kitchen desolate. "Tomás, the storm that's coming, that's not the Headache, is it?" I asked anxiously.

He forced a smile. "Spirits don't control the weather. God brings us the weather, right?"

But I was serious. "Don't go home. Stay here."

Because his chest hurt, he let me persuade him. My weather app said the snow would start before dawn.

I lay in my bed in the dark, aware that Tomás was on the bed in the guest room across the hall. I craved the protection of strong male arms to guard me against the evil that surrounded us, but I would not cross the hall and lie down with him. Was it indecent, an elderly woman cuddling with a man in his prime? Or was it unthinkable, like a mother spooning with her son? I didn't know, but I did know our friendship imposed boundaries. He was a priest, chaste and devoted to Christ, and I wasn't looking for love, as far as I knew. So I contented myself with Rayna's warm body against my back and Tomás across the hallway.

The ringing cell phone in the guest room woke me up. Be a misdial, I wished with all my heart, but I could hear the murmur of his voice. In a minute he opened my bedroom door and quietly spoke my name. Rolling to my side, I could see the dark of his form in the doorway.

"I was called by the parish. Mr. Taylor is ninety-two and they say he's dying."

My first cynical thought was that here was another person for Tomás to "save," although it was saving in the most narrow sense. My second cynical thought was that the Headache was luring Tomás, the chump, away from me and the voice. But if it was a death, I knew Tomás had to go.

"I'm coming back in the morning," he promised, and I let myself believe it.

Rayna went downstairs to see him off. As soon as she left the room, cold descended on me, chilling me from ears to toes. Getting up, I dressed in my warmest clothes: snow pants, heavy wool sweater, thick wool socks. I left my insulated hiking boots by the bed and crawled back under the covers. Even if the power went out, I'd probably stay warm.

Trotting back into the room, Rayna jumped on the bed and plunked down beside me. We could hear the stinging sound of new snow beating against the windows.

––––––––

First came pain, a headache slicing across my brain. Next came the nauseous cramps, making me retch. I woke up to gray light and the sound of claws scratching across the floor. The gray light was a blizzard whirling outside the bedroom windows, and the scratching claws belonged to a black beast that dashed back and forth along the bedroom wall.

Something hard and fat was prodding the tender interior of my brain. If I could only vomit it out, I'd feel better. Stomach heaving, I put my feet on the floor, intending to get to the toilet. But there was that raving devil near the door.

"Get out!" I screamed, "I'll kill you, bitch!" I could remember it was a dog I once loved, but now I needed to smash its head in.

Scanning the room for a weapon, I picked up an exercise barbell under the bedside table. I waved this above my head as I advanced on the creature. It stood like a rock, tail as thick as an iron bar, and I could feel its energy vibrate. Suddenly it vanished, and like a magic trick, now stared fiercely up at me from the bottom of the stairs.

In the toilet, I indulged in the thought of ripping the living flesh off the dog's bones and my stomach settled. When I peered at the mirror, I saw that my familiar face was old, pathetic, and ugly. Back in the bedroom, I laced up my hiking boots while I imagined kicking the dog to death.

I needed something better than a barbell to finish the dog off, something long I could swing hard. I pictured splitting the dog's head open, blood oozing from its skull and a dislodged eyeball dangling from the socket. There was a baseball bat somewhere in this house, and I found it in the room across the hall, where the bedspread was crumpled. Bile surged to my throat, I swung the bat, and shattered the bedside lamp. When I got to the top of the stairs the dog had disappeared, and I knew it would be hard to corner the bitch now.

Edging down the stairs, I held the bat across my body to ward off the beast's teeth. Outside the first floor windows, the world was a blank, swirling white, and when I opened the kitchen door, snow blew in on the gale. I left the door open and started to systematically search the downstairs for the dog. As I eased through doorways, I carried the bat loosely, to be ready. My brain throbbed, nausea turned my stomach, but my lust to beat the black thing to death was greater than my fear of it. When I slipped into the kitchen again, the wind wailing through the open door made it impossible to hear anything.

Something jumped straight at me from mid-air. Barely getting the bat between it and me, I pushed it sideways. It landed on four legs and backed slowly away, as the house rattled in the storm. The next instant the beast came at my ankle so fast I tripped and fell against the wall. It retreated again, confused by the smell of the boot. Getting my balance, I grasped the bat with sticky fingers, and settled into a crouch. Anticipation of the kill wet my mouth.

A flash of black motion and I swung hard enough to crack a skull. The creature sprang from the floor to meet me, closed its jaws around the bat and wrenched it from my hands. It hit the floor with the bat in its teeth and shot through the open door into the flying snow.

"Filth!" I shrieked, running after it.

I halted at the top of the back steps, because the black creature and bat had disappeared in the blowing white. Coming back to the kitchen, my killing lust was pulsing like interrupted sex. I slammed the door and kicked the nearest chair across the room. Then I sat in the other chair and visualized the dog writhing on the floor as I beat it to death with the bat.

Without warning, I leapt up and flung myself at the sink, vomiting up this hated presence. Relief filled my aching brain: Rayna was safe!

She was at home in the snow, and Tomás would find and keep her. With that joyful thought my mind shut down, and when I awoke, I was lying on the floor and seething with Headache's rage.

There was something I needed to destroy besides the dog, and it might be in this house. What it was I wasn't sure, but I'd know when I found it. I went upstairs to search the two back rooms, likely places for this thing to hide in. What I looked for was very cunning, but I was more powerful.

Starting in the room where the moving boxes were stored, I would pull open a box or closet and, standing perfectly still, smell for a whisper of energy. If I found nothing, I'd tear out all the contents, leaving them scattered in heaps on the floor. Now that I was free of the beast, I had to turn my whole attention to the search, in order to make the fat thing in my brain stop its insistent prodding. When I was done with boxes and closets, I left everything where it fell and went to what was supposed to be the playroom for grandkids—although I was confident there would never be grandkids in this house.

But I found nothing to kill in the back rooms and returned to the stairs. As I stepped out onto the first stair, my foot strayed out beyond the step and I was about to put my weight on empty space. Sensing the lack of resistance an instant before my foot plunged, I threw my body toward the stair railing. My arm shot out, my hand closing around a rail, my free hand grabbing the next rail, and my shins scraping the tread. I fetched up on my knees against the stair railing, holding onto the rails for dear life.

He wants to kill me! I thought. In the moment of free fall, or the dead-on grab that stopped me, my mind had sprung free. The Headache was in my brain, but my mind had autonomy.

Crowding the railing and waiting for my heart to settle, I realized my mind could watch him. He was hoping to see me tumble down the stairs and hurt myself. It would hurt him too, but that was part of his pleasure. Now I knew to keep away from the stove and the knives.

He wanted me on my feet so I complied, careful not to attract his attention by resisting. Something in him had shifted and he'd become more calculating, but it didn't appear he could read my mind or even wanted to. He was thirsty so we went into the kitchen, where, ignoring the smell of vomit, I sat sipping glasses of water and he entertained himself with visions of screaming people inside burning cars. Now I understood why Tomás had been afraid. Headache wasn't remotely human, he was elemental and harsh, a being fit for solar winds and airless space.

We both heard the car, crunching softly along the street through the blizzard. When it turned down the driveway, Headache became hyper-alert. We waited in silence, with no chorus of happy barks to welcome anyone.

Tomás walked in without knocking. He closed the door against the snow and stood without a word, maybe a little unsure of himself. I sat at the kitchen table, not knowing who looked out of my eyes. He glanced at the smelly sink and ran the water to clear it. Then he picked up the chair Headache had kicked over, set it upright, and hung his parka on the back. In suit jacket, black shirt, and clerical collar, he looked like the priest he was.

"Where's Rayna?" he asked lightly.

"If I ever see that fucking bitch again, I will rip it apart with my bare hands," I snarled. Well that settled who was doing the talking.

He sat down across from me. We looked at each other a long time, possibly because he was trying to find me somewhere in Headache's rage. Then he laid his hands flat on the table and bowed his head. In defeat? Certainly not in prayer.

Headache picked up the scent of victory. I growled, "Take off that fucking collar."

Tomás sat up and grabbed my wrists. I jumped, afraid Headache would electrocute him, but Tomás was in command. He had summoned his full authority and it lit up his eyes.

"Why do you threaten us?" he demanded.

"The old bag has something I need," I said. Headache was referring to me, of course.

"You're talking about my friend," Tomás angrily corrected him.

"She has something I want. Make her to give it to me."

"What does she have?"

Headache wasn't answering that one, I could feel his fear.

Tomás replied to the silence, "She decides, not me."

"She will suffer horribly. You would let me rip your friend apart?"

"The God I serve will protect her."

I exploded in a brutish laugh, spraying spit across the table. "Your little god is a pathetic, useless ass!"

Tomás went rigid. With an effort he loosened the hands that were crushing my wrists. "You have nothing to say about my God."

"Weak, helpless, and stupid, like all the rest. I know all the vain little gods and their silly stories. They contaminate the universe with their promises of hope and salvation. Their pitiful believers try so hard to please them and still suffer from birth to death." Headache made my voice harsh. "There is nothing the silly gods can do to alter what I do."

"What do you do?" Tomás challenged.

"I am one of the greater beings. We are principles of the universe. We determine what is possible. Because of me humans live lives of disappointment, sorrow, and pain."

"I see lives of faith and love," Tomás declared, as if his own life depended on it.

"You are deluded. You always have been."

"Don't you see goodness? Don't you see courage?"

"I see you wave your hands in the air and give people grape juice and stale bread to make them happy. I see you wasted your life."

Tomás breathed slowly, marshaling his power in the face of what, for him, must be monstrous lies. Then that look of his flashed—he understood.

"You are the principle of suffering."

Headache snorted, but didn't contradict.

"I was taught that suffering was noble," Tomás added with contempt.

"Suffering is abject and pitiful. Come back and see what happens to your old lady when she does not give me what I want. Listen to her scream for you when you are too weak to help."

"In our world, you are evil."

"Nothing as simple as that. There is a plane of energy that runs through the cosmos. It has no matter, time, or space. It is undetectable by your tools. It knits the cosmos together with the energy of being. I am an aspect of this energy."

"An aspect," Tomás echoed. "One aspect."

"More powerful than all your little gods together."

"I serve a great and loving God," Tomás declared.

His cell phone pinged.

"Mr. Taylor dies in fear and pain," Headache had me announce triumphantly. Tomás gave me a look of loathing and cast a glance at the text message. He stood up, grim with anger, and put on his parka.

"Just see what I can do!" I trilled with glee, and Headache jumped me up and threw me into the wall. My head hit with a solid crack and I started to slide to the floor. Tomás grabbed me and held me up, searching my face. Then he bent and kissed me on the cheek, a kiss meant for Headache and me. I was flooded with powerful, unearthly love. Headache gave a shriek and vanished.

At that moment I was absolutely certain the universe was good.

Tomás put me in the chair and hurried to the door. His last look asked for forgiveness.

———

All the rest of the short day the snow blew outside the cottage, while in the silence inside Headache wove himself back together. I gave no thought to breaking free, no leaping up to text Tomás, or braving the blizzard to shout for Rayna. Headache had taken possession and it wouldn't be easy to escape him, so my mind waited for his inevitable recovery. The kiss had blown him into disconnected fragments that occasionally issued a bleat to signal their existence, but eventually the fragments drew together into the fat, prodding energy I knew.

By late afternoon he'd gathered enough strength to start punching holes in the tissue of my brain. Or what felt like the tissue, not that it mattered. Areas of my head were bruised and raw, and with dread I understood that he was searching for the voice.

A sharp, physical stab of bladder pain brought me straight back to the present. I hurried across the hall to the bathroom, where, try as I might, I was unable to pee. I gave it up and reflexively washed my hands. When I saw my face in the mirror, beaming with hilarity, I grasped the awful dimensions of my situation. This was Headache's doing, he had found a simple and effective way to torture me.

Horror froze me. All those glasses of water I drank, my god, what was I thinking? I walked carefully through the kitchen to the dining room, to retrieve my phone. It still displayed the text message I'd sent to Tomás the previous evening, but when I touched the new message field, there was no cursor. Pressing the home button did nothing, and neither did pressing the power button. The phone was effectively frozen, just like on the afternoon Rayna ran away and almost got shot. Headache's laughter bounced around inside my brain and I sat down at the dining room table in despair. Maybe Headache couldn't control the weather, I thought bitterly, but he had plenty of other talents.

I never believed in Tomás' God, but I believed completely in Tomás. Damn Mr. Taylor for dying, I swore to myself, but quickly took it back because you can't blame an old man for dying. Besides, Mr. Taylor was probably suffering as much or more than I was. Remembering the remarkable kiss Tomás gave me, I wondered if his love and goodness had the power to help me. Or help Mr. Taylor. I squirmed on the chair, the aching sensation in my pelvis had increased and it was hard to get comfortable.

The floor looked like a better place to be, so I slid down beside the chair until I lay on my back. From here I could see the underside of the table and chairs, like a child. Closing my eyes, I thought about lying in the sun at the beach when I was a kid, and drifted in imagined warmth until the burning in my pelvis woke me up to the cold floor of a cottage in a blizzard. I would have called aloud to Tomás, but I remembered how Headache had taunted him and kept my mouth shut. So it was true, I had chosen horror and pain after all.

I considered crying out to Jesus, even though he was not and probably never would be my savior. Tomás had been my savior, and maybe he'd left a channel to Jesus open for me. I whispered, "Please, Jesus, help me," and it sounded pathetic. I tried shouting bravely, "Jesus, please help me!" but the silence gobbled up the sound and no help appeared. Instead, my pelvis burned hard and I wiped tears out of my eyes. I would die of this pain, abandoned in a freezing cottage.

Why was Headache torturing me like this? This was no pleasant entertainment of his, since he must be feeling the pain I suffered. For some reason he was trying to make me give the voice to him. Why that was necessary was a puzzle to solve later, but all I knew for certain was, if he waited for me to give up the voice, he'd have to wait forever. Then I caught the whisper of a thought: His strategy required his full attention. If he took his attention off me for an instant, my bladder would release. As long as he froze my bladder in pain, he couldn't search for the voice, and my precious voice was safe.

Ah, so simple! It was my task to protect the voice and I could do this because I loved the voice. Love gave my suffering courage and my body strength. Feeling a grace I'd never known, I saw it all, how I would save the voice and if I died, Tomás would take Rayna and they'd be happy. I thought of Bill, lying on his side on the bed in a half-dark room. The skin on his hands was soft and delicate, still slightly warm, but his feet had turned cold as the furnace of life shut down. His eyes were closed and his thin mouth moved without sound. Maybe he was telling me all the things he might have said over the years. I stroked his living hands.

I leaned down and scooped up the little black puppy, setting her beside me on the couch. She pressed her whole body against my side and tucked her black-velvet muzzle up behind my ear. Resting her chin on my shoulder, she gave a soft puppy sigh and fell asleep. Over and over, I played this sequence in my mind, while my body contended with pain.

It was full dark when Headache made me move. I was in intense pain, but I knew if I could get out of the house and into the car, the pain would stop. Headache and I were very clear on this. I turned on my stomach, close to fainting, and inched along the floor until I was in the kitchen. There the back door stumped me, until I managed to use the cabinet beside the door to pull myself up. On its top were my gloves and car keys, where I always left them. With my gloves on and clutching the keys, I pulled open the door and toppled onto my knees, into the snow at the top of the steps.

The heavy snowfall had given way to a light, steady snow blowing sideways in the wind. The back stairs were covered in drifts, but the driveway was passable. Get in the car and the pain will stop, I promised myself. A line of frigid snow dropped from the second floor down the back of my sweater, propelling me to the bottom of the stairs. In the driveway, I panted and crawled around the car until I could kneel by the driver's door. The handle was level with my face and I was able to yank it open with my left hand. Now I had to get into the driver's seat.

Hands shaking, I laid the keys on the center console and stopped to rest. Then I grabbed the steering wheel, took a breath, and cried out as I hauled myself up. I was aware of Headache's impatience. He was disgusted with how long this was taking and probably gave me strength I didn't have. I lay against the steering wheel to collect myself, got the key in the ignition, and backed blindly into the street. It would be over soon.

Violent gusts of wind periodically wrapped the car in white-outs. I drove, not caring where I went. Headache knew where we were going.

We were approaching a turn when a sudden gust hit the car, the windshield went solid white, and the world outside vanished. With no intention of mine I floored the gas, the car leapt from the road, and bounced off something solid. At the moment of impact, my bladder let loose.

In the quiet of the stopped car, I could see the tree I hit. Soaked from the waist down, I began to pound my fists on the steering wheel and shout with joy.

A Bad Night at the Beach

Headache wasn't pleased at all, and had me beat my head against the steering wheel. It didn't bother me, because I was as happy as a redeemed sinner. Jesus hadn't come to rescue me, and God's divine goodness hadn't thrown the car into a tree, but something had intervened. Something greater and wiser than I could imagine, with perfect timing and the ability to see through snow.

As soon as Headache was done bashing my forehead on the wheel, I opened the car door and fell into a soft bed of snow. The squalls had died down, the air was cold enough to bite, and I knew he wasn't through with me yet, but I wasn't alone any more and that changed everything. As I lay in the snow, I realized I'd never been alone, not during this awful day, and not since August when I first heard the voice in the static.

Except I'd been wrong about the voice—it wasn't a "he."

I tried to keep my mind blank so Headache wouldn't recognize my joy. The crash happened in seconds and Headache's attention had been fixed on my bladder, which was the genius of her plan. She found a way to intervene without revealing herself. Did he guess she'd helped me, and could he feel her goodness?

Now he wanted me to walk along the street and I did. My bladder ached with residual pain but it was nothing, because I was no longer his toy to destroy however he wanted. Her presence brought knowledge, which I digested as I trudged through the snow. I'd been right, in order for Headache to destroy the voice, I had to force her from where she hid in my thoughts. Then he could grab her and eat her, or something equally horrible. But if I chose to die protecting her, she would escape him. She was beautiful and subtle and vastly powerful, and she needed me. Of course I would die for her.

I hoped there wouldn't be much suffering involved, and I was very grateful Rayna was nowhere near us, because I couldn't stand to see her suffer. Although, I remembered, the voice had only mentioned horror and pain, so perhaps my death wouldn't be required. She was probably weaker than Headache, which is why she needed to hide with me. He could do what he wanted, freeze cell phones, blast Tomás, and hurt Mr. Taylor, while she had to stay hidden.

It was no surprise to discover Headache was taking me to the beach. My wet pants had turned cold but still provided insulation, and my strength increased from knowing she was with me. How odd, I thought, it was like the strength Tomás must feel from Jesus. Was I experiencing a religious conversion without the religion?

In the beach parking lot, the snow was up to my knees and I had to slog my way through it to reach the marsh. There the wind ruled and swept the sand clean of snow. My pants and boots were adequate, but my thick wool sweater was no protection at all from the wind. We'd better get on with this before I freeze to death, I thought, but maybe that's what Headache wanted, a slow and fearful death in the wind. From the bluff, the ocean was black as ink, with gray spume flying off the waves in tattered clumps. The last time I'd been here it was a sunny morning and I'd been terrified. Now in the dark and cold, I was even more afraid.

Headache wanted me to go down the bluff and I refused. He was in a hurry and didn't bother with pain, instead he stopped my breathing. Lungs crying for air, I waved my arms wildly and pitched down the slope, rolling over rocks until I slammed my knee on a boulder at the bottom. As I lay over the boulder, sucking air like a dying fish, I felt a murderous rage begin to grow. It was not Headache's rage, it was a rage all my own.

My mind became crystal clear. There was only one place Headache wanted me tonight. I'd been in cold water in many triathlons, but never as cold as this would be. I knew you might have ten minutes before your core temperature dropped and you weakened, which meant maybe five minutes of useful swimming. Night was a hazard, especially with the grinding rocks at the lower end of the beach. My life depended on staying up at this end where the bottom was sandy.

My gloves would hinder swimming and my boots would drag me down, but the thick socks could be useful if the footing was stony.

I got up and limped out on the sand, where I took off my gloves and boots, leaving both above the tide line. They would tell Tomás where I disappeared, and along with the open cottage door and the crashed car, he'd put together the story.

I was counting on Headache not knowing I could swim, so I could surprise him and somehow save my life. I kept my thoughts firmly away from the voice. He would not scare me into revealing her, I would call on Tomás instead. The light snow had stopped and the wind was blowing the clouds apart. Headache walked me across the frozen sand and into the water.

The cold was stunning. My feet and legs immediately went numb and I couldn't feel the bottom. At every cautious step through the water, questions. Am I veering toward the rocks? How far will Headache make me walk? The icy water climbed up my body as it came in and fell away as it went out. What will make Headache quit? When will I get a chance to swim? Far out on the water I saw a dark swell rising and my stomach clenched.

The ocean topped my shoulders and I began to hyperventilate in quick, urgent breaths. I knew about this too and stopped moving to let it pass. It seemed like stopping was my idea, but when I tried to steady myself against the moving water, my foot wouldn't respond. Then my right leg—no, it was both legs—were as inert as rocks. The distant swell had formed into a large black wave that was coming ashore. My arms, now in the water, now out, hung solid in the air. Headache had paralyzed me.

Rage burst from me, splitting the night sky. "You fucking bastard!" I screamed to the heavens. "You can't kill me like this!"

The night lit up with daylight.

Bright as noontime, I saw a white crest gathering on the blue wave as it swept toward me. Free to move, I turned my back on it and crouched. As the lip swept over me, I jumped and was drawn to the top. With my eyes locked on the beach, I lay flat and swam for all I was worth. The wave carried me to the shore and threw me down under crushing turbulence. With no up or down, I tumbled in the water's force until my shoulder hit sand and my face scraped grit. The wave pushed me up the beach until my body stuck on the sand.

The foaming water fell away from me, rushing forward, but soon it was back, tugging me to join it in the ocean. I dug my fingers in the sand and hung on until it slipped away, then crawled as fast as I could to get out of the water. I kept going until I was half way to the bluff, where I collapsed in the freezing wind.

She would not let me stay there. Shivering violently in the cold sunlight, I struggled on to the bottom of the bluff. In my mind I could see, as if it was only a little ways away, a sheltered hollow at the edge of the marshes, a stand of tall stalks and grasses where deer might lie down. She wanted me there, so on hands and knees I clambered up the bluff, and crept, head down in the wind, over the scree at the top. When I snuck between the brittle stalks into the center of the hollow, day flicked back to night. Drawing my legs up to my chest, I buried my hands in my armpits, and fell into a sleep where black-legged animals circled me all night long.

Something woke me. It was still night, but Tomás had stuck his cell in the sand for light. He was wrapping me in his parka, and tears ran down his cheeks.

"Stop it," I croaked, "don't cry. She was with me."

He wiped his sleeve across his face apologetically. With my arms inside the parka, he zipped it up to my chin, tightened the hood, and prepared to pick me up and carry me.

"No," I said as clearly as I could, "I want to walk."

With a doubtful look, he stood and reluctantly pocketed his phone. Then he hoisted me to my feet and let me lean against him.

My mouth close to his ear, I whispered my secret. "Tomás, she made the daylight!"

I had so much to tell him.

———

The next time I woke, it was dawn. I was in bed and there was a woman in my bedroom. I attempted to roll over and sit up, but a spasm of pain seized my back and made me yelp.

"Now wait, let me help you," the woman warned, hurrying over.

With authority she leaned me forward, deftly stacked pillows behind me, and settled me again. She must be a nurse, I thought, and recognized her as Janice.

"I have arthritis in my back," I rasped, but arthritis was hardly my problem. I remembered being pounded by icy water, and now I was hot and weak.

"It's a wonder you could walk at all," Janice declared. "Father Thomas told me you insisted on walking to the parking lot in your socks."

That sounded about right. I couldn't remember much, except he'd been crying when he found me.

"He had to go back to the parish," Janice explained. "Mr. Taylor passed last night. Everything happens at once."

But now I wasn't paying attention, because Rayna was nowhere on the bed. I twisted my head to look around the room. So early in the morning, she had to be there. Then I remembered why she wasn't.

"Can I get you something?" Janice asked.

You can get me my dog, I thought, but had no idea what to say. What had Tomás told her? What could he tell her?

"No, I'm all right," I murmured.

She shook some pills into her hand and I recognized the bottle from two days ago, when Rayna followed me through the cottage, so fierce and bereft. The next day, just yesterday, she disappeared into the snow with a baseball bat in her teeth. Janice handed me the pills and a cup of water. It made absolutely no sense that I was alive and Rayna was still missing.

"You know, you'd have gone straight to the hospital if you hadn't been walking," she remarked. "But you did walk and you had all your fingers, so he brought you back here."

Heart aching for Rayna, I handed her the empty cup.

"You're not half as frozen as I'd have thought. He must have come on you right off," Janice said, with obvious admiration.

If Tomás had seen Rayna, would she come to him? Would she refuse to enter the house because of Headache's smell?

"When will he be back?" I asked.

"I'm sure by the end of the day. He's got the Taylor family and then the prison. Do you want to use the bathroom? Or could you sleep some more?"

A whole day—much too long to wait. The words rushed out, "Did he say anything about my dog?"

"Oh no, is the dog gone too?"

"In the snow," I answered vaguely.

"I'll keep an eye out for it when I'm downstairs. It's very hard, losing an animal, but I bet it comes back. They mostly do."

I shut my eyes, aching, hot, wondering how it was possible Rayna wasn't sleeping beside me.

It was midday and sunny by the time I woke again. Janice had brought the bedroom armchair closer to the bed and settled herself in it with a magazine. Now she told me how much better I looked. I moved my legs experimentally, discovering they were stiff but working, and I no longer felt hot.

"I can get up now," I said, reaching out for her hand.

In the bathroom mirror, my hair stood up stiff with salt water and abrasions ran across one side of my face. When I got in the shower, I noticed that I had a swollen knee that was well on its way to turning purple. That was when I crashed into the rock and became enraged, I recalled, a rage so pure it was almost holy.

Standing under the warm water, I went over what had happened the night before. She gave me the rage to defend myself, she made me crawl up to the grassy hollow, she got Tomás to the beach to find me before I froze. And the thing she did with the daylight . . . . It filled me with awe to remember.

But what about Rayna, why hadn't she come home? Surely last night was the end of the conflict between Headache and the Voice, the Voice had triumphed, and Rayna should be back with me. Combing out the mess of my hair, I decided to eat lunch and then go out to look for her. Janice obviously wasn't a dog person, but I guessed I could persuade her to search with me.

Janice had brought up some sandwiches and left them on my bedside table. I took clean clothes out of the dresser and sat on the bed to dress before I ate. The moment I was off my feet, the energy left my body. Trying to remove my robe, I discovered my hand was too weak to grasp the cloth. I let the hand fall and watched the colors of the room fade around me. I barely made it back under the covers before I was buried by sleep.

I woke at dusk. The light on the bedside table was on and I lay still, surveying the bedroom. Rayna wasn't there but Janice seemed comfortable enough, reading in the armchair.

Noticing I was awake, she rose to help me, but this time I sat up on my own. When I agreed I was hungry, she brought the sandwiches back and sat down to chat while I ate. She told me how the plow guys had come on my car during the night. It was in the shop now, but she doubted I'd get it back before Christmas. I said that was ok, my kids would be here in . . . , and stared at her blankly. Together we worked out that there were three days until my family arrived.

Then she settled back in the chair and addressed me with a sober expression. "Well, what on earth went on last night?"

She was bound to ask, a person like her. Could I say an evil spirit came, grabbed my dog, and threw me in the ocean? The dog was missing and it was pretty obvious I'd been in the water, but Janice wouldn't go for evil spirits. I wondered if she knew just how strange her friend Father Thomas could be.

I asked as casually as I could, "What did Father Thomas tell you?"

"He said he went to look in on you during the storm, but there was no car in the driveway. He had an idea you might be at the beach, and went out there. Actually, how he put it was Jesus told him to look for you at the beach, and who's to say that's not true? You were awfully lucky."

I could picture Tomás driving in the driveway, the house dark, the kitchen door open with snow blowing in. He'd rush through the house, throwing on all the lights, then get back in his car, certain now that I'd be in the place I was forbidden to go. He'd pass my crashed car with its open door, and take a moment to check inside. That would confirm to him where I'd gone.

I tried to keep my answer to Janice's question general, but believable. "I wanted to see the waves in the storm. I slipped on the rocks at the far end, and then I had to fight my way back to shore."

She nodded. I could see huge problems with my story, chief of which was: Why did I still go to the beach after I crashed the car? But she had another thought in mind.

"How were you feeling the days before the storm came? Were you down? Sad?"

Alert nurse that she was, she asked the real questions. And no, I couldn't claim I'd been well-adjusted and happy. I'd been panicked, confused, agitated, and a host of other things I couldn't even name. Feeling very emotional, I blinked away a tear. It was the effect of my miraculous rescue from the ocean, no doubt.

Struggling to smile, I assured her, "I wasn't trying to hurt myself, I promise you. I left Boston for a lot of reasons, but it's been ok up here. Father Thomas has been a good friend." The last, at least, was believable.

"Good your family is coming so soon, I bet that'll be nice for you."

"I hope so," I said, although I wasn't entirely sure they'd be safe. And then there was Rayna, or the lack of Rayna. "I need to find my dog before they come. You know, the grandkids . . . . Can you help me? I have to get outside to look for her."

"Of course you do, but not in the dark. Wait for Father Thomas, he'll have some ideas. Now hang on a bit, I'm going to fix your face," and she got up to leave the room.

I was thinking how hard it was to wait for Tomás, when Janice returned with a bowl of water and other things for my face. Working by the bedside light, she began to clean the grit out of my cheek.

"At least you got this in clean, cold salt water. Not off a grimy frozen highway."

I kept still while she applied ointment to the abrasions. The ointment felt better than the air.

"Father Thomas said you were in quite a state when he found you. He doesn't know how you got yourself up to the marshes, but he said you were curled up in the grass like a little animal." Giving me a significant look, she added, "He was very concerned to find you like that."

She meant that Tomás thought I'd died, and I felt all the emotion of the last two days crowd my heart.

After she taped gauze over my cheek, she gave my face a critical appraisal in the bedside light. "What's all these bruises on your forehead? Did you hit your head on the rocks?"

"That's from driving into the tree," I replied, hurrying on. "Janice, do you think you could look at my knee? I fell down chasing Rayna." I shoved my purple knee out from under the covers.

"Rayna's a pretty name," Janice observed, turning her attention to my knee.

Tomás arrived an hour later and I heard him slowly climb the stairs. His arrival allowed Janice to leave, and he waited at the bedroom door while she gave me instructions on keeping quiet and caring for my face and knee. She wished me a warm and happy Christmas with my family and my dog, and the two of them went downstairs, no doubt discussing the state of my health.

He returned a few minutes later with my boots and gloves, which he deposited by the dresser. He'd probably been two days without sleep, and looked wasted. Sinking into the armchair, he dropped his head in his hands. I thought he might be taking a quick nap, but when I heard a murmur of Spanish I realized this was prayer. In the deep silence of the room, it felt intimate to be included in his devotions. I wondered if I was more like him now, after I'd experienced the greatness of the Voice and the miracle of daylight.

When he finally raised his head, I asked, "What did you pray for?"

"They were prayers of gratitude."

"For Mr. Taylor who went to heaven?"

"And for you, who didn't." He gave a wan smile.

Don't pray about me, I thought, Rayna's the one who's missing. "Rayna ran away when Headache chased her around the house with a baseball bat. Next time you pray, ask for her to come back."

He didn't seem concerned. "Maybe she has something she needs to do."

"I need her with me."

"She'll come home when she can."

"You can't possibly know that."

"Ok, I don't know," he said defensively. He pointed at the boots and gloves, "I brought those back. I found them on the beach this morning—where you left them for me." He knew I'd been prepared to die.

"How much did I tell you last night?"

"You were pretty crazy. You looked like one of those wild-eyed saints and you kept telling me she made the daylight. Also you limped to the car in your socks."

"The limping was from my knee. I smashed it on a rock when Headache made me fall down the bluff."

He averted his face as if he didn't want to hear any more. I decided to keep my story short.

"Headache was trying to make me give up the Voice, so he walked me into the ocean. I took off my boots first because I was planning to swim, but he paralyzed me just as a massive wave came in. He wanted me to see my death and betray her."

Tense, Tomás waited on my words.

"But Tomás, I cursed him. I screamed at the sky. That's when she turned night into day!" I felt the thrill of it all over again.

He was shaking his head, eyes lit. "No, it was you. You made the daylight."

"That's not true." I frowned at him, "You do know who I'm talking about?"

"Of course, I know," he sighed. "You're not talking about the Blessed Mother."

Suddenly, all my grief caught up with me. "Great beyond belief, Tomás!" I cried in a broken voice. "As good as you are good!" I started to sob.

Exhausted, he rose from the chair and hovered there.

"I would have died to save her!" I wailed to him. "Now I don't even know if she lives!"

"It's not over yet. That's why Rayna's not home."

"But why isn't it over? She won, Headache lost. How long? Days? Weeks? Because my heart's going to break without Rayna, without her—."

I was stopped by a vision of myself, a gray-haired woman with gauze taped over her cheek, crying in the light of a bedside lamp. The woman thought she was suffering the loss of the ones she loved, but she had no idea. There was a much bigger context. Headache and the Voice, whatever they were, were contending over her. They were contending with her.

I sat up straight.

"What?" Tomás wanted to know.

I seemed to have lost my breath. "I have a part, I've been playing it," I panted. Now I was dizzy and lay back on the pillows.

He watched me intently. When I got my breath, I said, "Tomás, go home and get some sleep."

"What did you see?"

"I don't know yet. Go home, you look wretched. Take care of yourself."

Christmas Dreams

Rayna was never a dog to bark at the door to be let in, she was too self-sufficient. The next morning I installed myself on the living room couch, where I could hear the jingle of a collar or movement at the door. The snow cover was two feet deep, but my driveway had been plowed and the back stairs shoveled. Someone had cleaned up the debris of Headache's invasion, probably an exhausted Tomás or I would have had some difficult questions from Janice.

Unbelievably, the next day was the winter solstice and my family was arriving the second day after it. We'd had nice Christmases when the kids were little and I liked the holiday, but I was no longer a mother or grandmother, or even a retired mental health counselor. My position in the world had shifted, although I couldn't say how. But it was too late to undo the Christmas plans and I did yearn for my family, so I sent off an email with the same flimsy story I told Janice. Within minutes the phone rang, and long phone calls ensued, in which I declared I was all right and tried to stay positive about finding Rayna.

That evening I got a phone call from a sweet sounding, older woman. Apparently, Father Thomas had suggested that after my accident, I could use some help getting things in for the holiday. I told her what I really needed was help looking for my dog, and she said that was also possible. On the afternoon of the solstice, four ladies and a gentleman stood in my driveway, breathing small clouds of vapor into the sunlight as they plotted their strategy. The searchers intended to cover ground, so I went with the shoppers, noticing that now I perfectly fit the image of an invalid shut-in.

But on coming home from shopping, I was completely unprepared for the anguish that seared my heart as I unlocked the door of a silent house. Later the searchers returned with no good news, and I promised myself I wouldn't go out again, until either Rayna was back or I'd given up finding her. I had already notified local vets, the police, and the microchip database, so there wasn't much left to do except get the cottage ready for the families.

Hobbling upstairs to look at the playroom, I stopped to touch the stair railing and wonder about the wisdom of having my kids and grandkids visit me here. If I tried to ask the Voice about this, would a hoard of Headaches erupt, with no more Rayna to protect me? Standing on the stairs, I closed my eyes and waited for a warning. When none showed up, I waited for some type of reassurance. For the moment, the cottage seemed safe enough, so I put my trust in the Voice, and went on upstairs. In the back rooms, I discovered that Tomás had folded the clothes and sorted the shoes and games, before he put them away.

The next morning I watched the sunrise from my bed. It took a different kind of courage to wake up every day to a day without Rayna, than it took to walk into the freezing ocean. You either did or didn't walk into the ocean, but how do you tolerate the lie of a sunrise that promises new hope each morning? All day long I reminded myself that Rayna was missing, not dead, but once it got dark I lost the distinction between the two.

I thought back to the image of the woman in bed, experiencing a loss that was insignificant compared to the huge space surrounding her. I was willing to accept that in this giant space I could survive the loss of Rayna, but really, all I wanted was the small space of Rayna's warm body pressing against my back at night.

My beautiful Voice remained silent, and after some thought I realized the miracle of daylight was not a celestial event, and the Earth did not discover noontime in the middle of a December night. It was a trick of perception, a sudden increased sensitivity to light, similar to the way animals can see in the dark. It was sad how I had no talent for believing in the extraordinary.

———

———

The families flew east all that day, stayed overnight in Boston, and drove up the next morning in a rental van. They had gotten rooms in a motel so the kids would have a swimming pool, and they went there first. Then the whole pile of them, four adults and three kids, bundled into the van and came to the cottage. First in the kitchen door was Emily, in tears before she reached me.

"Oh my god, Mom," she sobbed, "You look ok, you do! But Rayna," she whispered, "what are we going to do without Rayna?" We wept and clung together while the others crowded into the kitchen behind her. Wiping her eyes, Emily pulled me toward the cluster of grandkids by the door.

"Look, guys," she told them, "Nana's fine! People here think she's a superhero!"

I wasn't exactly fine, with a cheek decorated by red streaks like war paint, but little Davie came and flung his arms around my waist. Cara and Susan held back, staring at me apprehensively. Perhaps it was the unnatural quiet without Rayna, or the way I looked, or the odd story of my falling in the ocean on a stormy winter night. Still, I wasn't raising faint-hearted grandchildren, so I advanced on the girls.

"If you think this is bad," I pointed to my cheek, "you should see this . . . ," and lifting my pant leg, I exposed a lurid yellow and purple flower blooming around my knee. Cara and Susan squealed, squeezing my hands in delight, and I supposed the visit might go ok after all.

My son David, his wife Chris, and Emily's husband Phil, came to hug me one by one. Their faces expressed a mixture of sadness and worry, each probably doubtful that they could muster enough happiness to float this holiday. Then everyone scattered, running up the stairs, trying the leather chairs in the living room, and admiring the cast iron bathtub in the bathroom. I followed, discovering in every room that Rayna wasn't there.

That night I dreamt the wolf dream once more. She followed the same route through the big trees and crept under the same fallen logs. The hemlock saplings cast the same spiky shadows, and the light on the snow changed from bright to milky white as she entered the forest. As the dream continued and the gray wolf loped up a steep grade, I felt excited anticipation. She came out on an open rocky ridge and vanished into a dense stand of wind-stunted trees.

Waking in the dark, I was thrilled that the Voice was speaking to me again. And better, the wolf had run to the top of a mountain, almost above the tree line—this might be the day Rayna came back! I peered around the bedroom to make sure she wasn't already there, then settled under the covers to snooze until daylight. It was Christmas eve day and all morning I floated in optimism, ready to hear the jingle of her collar and open the door.

The family arrived late morning and we herded the kids upstairs to play. Phil and Chris went to the kitchen to start lunch, while David, Emily, and I sat in the living room. I listened to stories about grand-children accomplishments that had once fascinated me, the basketball games and art classes, swimming lessons and school chorus, that were now so insubstantial compared with the events of my life.

After a while David got up to check on the chefs in the kitchen. Emily leaned forward, laying a kindly hand on my good knee.

"Chris and I walked on the beach this morning. It's pretty, in a windswept kind of way. We met a guy about your age, he was quite decent looking. He told us he lives on the edge of the marsh, so we gave him a detailed description of Rayna. He's going to set out food, you know, in case she's hanging out there."

"That's very nice of him," I said, thinking that it was more likely she was in the spruce forest across the driveway.

"Mom, we are all so sorry!" Emily burst out, jumping up to embrace me for a full minute, to show how much everyone cared. She sat back down and blew her nose. "Do you think she's just out having fun, like looking for mice under the snow?"

"It's possible. I feel hopeful today."

"You're very brave. This hasn't been a good place for you."

"We don't know that yet." It wasn't even lunchtime, and there was a whole afternoon for Rayna to come home.

"Phil and I were talking. We decided we want you to come out and stay with us."

This was no surprise. "For a visit?"

"For as long as you want."

But this was new. "Oh honey, that's very sweet of you."

She gazed at me, fully aware I wasn't enthusiastic about the invitation. "We were going to ask you anyway, before, you know, Rayna."

"Let's talk about it once Rayna gets home," I suggested, hoping that wouldn't be so far away.

In the long pause, I knew she didn't want to inform me that the chances of Rayna coming back were declining daily. "Sure, Mom, it's a hard time. We can wait."

Hearing her disappointment, I had to ask. "What?"

"Well, the way work is going . . . you know the project's about finished . . . ." Her expression hovered between excited and sorrowful.

I must have looked puzzled, because she suddenly exclaimed, "It's probably our last good chance, Mom!"

Oh, I thought, yes, it was puzzling. This must be about having a baby, but it was a bad time to have that conversation with her mother. In a lightening calculation, I weighed whether a new grandchild would make up for the loss of Rayna. Not a chance.

I wasn't so selfish that I'd ignore her happiness, so I smiled broadly and exclaimed, "Cara and Susan will love that!" Then both of us were shedding tears over Rayna again.

Blotting her eyes, Emily said, "It'll be such a help if you're out there."

"Let's see how it goes," I replied, imagining how I would open the cottage door after dark and see Rayna separate herself from the night.

"Just don't wait too long, Mom," she warned me. "You'll break your heart."

"Maybe she has a job to do," I volunteered.

"God, Mom, don't say that, it sounds crazy."

———

The next morning was Christmas Day, and once again the sun rose brightly on a house without Rayna. After yesterday's failure to produce Rayna, I felt it was time to begin the long haul, that somber dance between hope and resignation. I was glad when the motel crowd arrived to distract my attention from the empty white landscape outside.

For that day and the next we ate and drank, played games, watched Netflix, and demonstrated, for anyone who cared, how to have a happy Christmas. The parents were understanding and the kids were kind and considerate. I suspected everyone was relieved to return to the motel at night, where they could jump, yell, and squabble, with nothing to remind them of dogs, missing or otherwise. I went to bed dulled by wine and sugar and had no wolf dreams.

Two days after Christmas, the four adults walked around town, asking folks to watch out for a black dog that looked like a fox. I kept indoors and played with the kids, questioning when I'd be ready to brave the sadness that lurked for me outdoors. By this time, I accepted the families' visit as a pause in the conflict between Headache and the Voice. It was an eye blink in the greater beings' existence, allowing my family to come and go unharmed. I was fairly confident that my family wouldn't be consumed in a fiery crash on their way back to California.

Rayna, on the other hand, was an essential element of the conflict. For the Voice, she was my spirit, and for Headache, she was his nemesis. I began to hope that my family's departure would return Rayna to me, so that she and I could complete what the Voice wanted. Then the great contest would be over, and Rayna and I would resume our normal lives.

Tomás came to meet my family at the end of their visit. The man who arrived at my door was not the strange priest with glittering eyes, but a good-looking Latino guy who shook hands warmly. We drank coffee in the living room, chatting about the differences between LA, Chicago, and Boston. Phil had gone to school in Chicago, and he and Tomás discovered a mutual passion for the Chicago Fire soccer team. Not one of us mentioned Rayna or my fall in the ocean.

Eventually people drifted off, David and Chris to check on the kids upstairs, and Tomás and Phil to watch Chicago Fire replays on the internet. Emily and I were alone in the kitchen, stacking dirty cups in the sink.

She turned to me with a dramatic pause. "Celibate and too young, but otherwise not a bad pick."

We were hooting with laughter, when Phil came in from the hall. "Em, go look at Lee's brain drawings. They're pretty funny!"

Damn, I thought, I meant to put them away.

"I liked the one with the little people in the valleys and the voices coming out of the doors," Phil told me. "But I'm not sure Tomás knew what to make of them."

When we went back to the living room, Tomás had a fixed, stoic expression. Before I could cross the room to speak to him, a screech of indignation came from upstairs. Shrill and angry voices indicated that kindness and consideration had been all used up for this holiday. Phil trooped upstairs with Tomás in tow, and was soon herding kids down to mingle with the adults. It was a while before I realized Tomás hadn't come with them.

He was sitting alone on the guest room bed, contemplating the table where the bedside lamp used to stand.

"I was going to get you a new light," he said morosely.

"Don't worry, nobody's using the room now."

"No, no one is," he said resentfully.

"What's the matter?"

"The drawings. You're right, you were an idiot."

My legs felt so tired, I had to sit on the bed, but I was very careful not to touch him. "I'm sorry, Tomás. When I did them I was desperate."

He shut his eyes, covering his face with his hand. "It's all I think about, leaving you with Headache. I know you survived—but the vomit, the pieces of glass, you sleeping in the snow with just a sweater . . . ." He dropped his hand and looked at me with open anger. "I can't forgive myself, how weak I was."

"You had to go. You aren't someone who could abandon Mr. Taylor."

"I did shit for him too."

He was a defeated man, blaming himself for what he couldn't control. Having nothing I could say to help him, the two of us sat without speaking until we heard a general stirring downstairs. People moved around, and kids went past our door on their way to the play-room. Putting on his guest face, for the next hour Tomás did an excellent impersonation of the good priest who aids the afflicted.

The following day, the van stopped for a final good-bye on its way to Boston. Although I'd been alone every night of their visit, I could see how worried the adults were to leave me. Chris thought she'd fly east next month so the two of us could do Portland together. Emily said I should come out there as soon as I was free, "free" being a tricky word I didn't want to explore. But I took all their love and put it up in my heart against the hard times that were surely coming. Watching them traipse down the kitchen steps and climb back in the van, I felt a tangle of gratitude, love, and sorrow.

At nine that evening Tomás called me, saying he wanted to take me someplace we could talk. This was peculiar since we'd been talking since October, but maybe he wanted to go to a church to talk about Headache. Instead we drove north along the coast and ended up at a tavern, a squat two-story building with white Christmas lights around its windows.

Tomás held the door for me to enter this place where I never expected he would go. It was hot compared to the cold outside, and crowded with customers. Guys wore big parkas while the women had far too little on their legs for the weather. We squeezed past the standing people and threaded our way around the ones who were sitting, until we reached a small table pushed against the wall.

"What are we doing in a bar?" I asked, sounding like a critical mother. We hadn't said anything on the way up, and he didn't bother to answer me.

The waitperson leaned over and Tomás asked for three shots of tequila. So that was what we were doing. When she put three shot glasses in front of him, he picked up one and set it before me. Then he lifted one of his glasses, saluted me, and knocked it back. Setting down the empty glass, he picked up his second one.

"Oh come on!" I protested.

"I used to be pretty good at this," he replied, meaning good at downing shots, I assumed. I reached over, taking the glass from his hand, and saw I was looking at a drowning man.

I'd seen drowning men and women in my career, so I adjusted my expression and said pleasantly, "I suppose that was in Peru."

For an answer, he picked up the glass in front of me and drank it straight down. I held on to the one in my hand, wondering if we were going to end up wrestling over it.

"Why are you getting drunk?"

"Because you unleashed evil on the world."

"I did?"

"Rayna's gone. Mr. Taylor died a hard death. Only the Lord Christ knows what you suffered. All the lights were off but the kitchen door was open. I went through all the rooms before I knew where you were. By the time I got there, I could just see this line of broken snow going up to the marsh. In another ten minutes it would have been gone. You came this close to dying," and he thrust at me a thumb and forefinger pressed hard together.

I sat quiet as a stone, and when he held out his hand for the last full glass, I drew it closer to my chest.

"Yesterday I saw what you did." His voice was getting louder. "You brought Headache into the house, you invited him in. Maybe She wanted you to do that. Maybe my God is a useless ass, I don't know."

Pain pinched my heart. I let him have the shot glass.

Holding my gaze, he emptied the glass. There was more to report. "I was at the prison today. Darnell was raped. It's pretty rare here, but it happens. No one much cares, except Darnell and me."

The poor kid, I thought, twenty-five years inside and the rest of his life outside, to try to come to terms with the cruelty. Was this chain of suffering my fault? The Voice was hidden, Headache was ascendant.

I did the driving back to the cottage, and made Tomás come in with me so I wouldn't feel the silence hiding in the corners. He didn't want to sober up and refused coffee, choosing to drive to the parsonage as he was. I half hoped he'd cross paths with the rector and they would have a real heart-to-heart, but then, there was too much that couldn't be said.

The next morning I went on the internet, hoping to find solace in the beauty of NGC 300. Older stars hung in the misty yellow-green pinwheel at the center, young hot stars clumped along the spiral arms in bright blue ultraviolet clouds, and pink smudges marked heated gas and supernova explosions. But it only made me sad. The galaxy was so beautiful, while down here on Earth everything was going to shit. Rayna was lost, and in his own way, so was Tomás. Mr. Taylor was harmed and so was Darnell. Who was to say goodness was not extinguished from the world?

Picking up after my visitors, my mind began to drift. It felt as though the space inside the cottage was expanding. As I tidied the rooms, I began to see flickers of forest light in the corners of my eyes. Occasionally some trick of vision would convince me the wolf's forest was inside the cottage and I'd turn sharply to catch a glimpse of the wolf—but it was only the familiar cottage. At first this visual trickery annoyed me, then it made me anxious. Finally, I went to the dining room for my drawing materials and sat down at the oak table to draw.

My recall of the wolf dreams was fast and accurate, so that scenes materialized on paper with hardly any effort. Soon the wolf was climbing the slope through the trees and running out onto the open ledge. But still more images came, as she wound her way down through the tree line, and further down into a forested valley. It was early summer in the valley and bright green ash leaves cast dappled shadows across the forest floor. She tracked among the shadows, moving fast from one trace of blood to the next. Then I was startled by the sound of leaves rustling inside the cottage, and the sigh of wind in nonexistent pine branches. I dropped my pencil in alarm and watched as it rolled across the floor.

My cell rang. Tomás. Good, I thought, he better be sober.

"Well how are you?" I wanted to know, but he wasn't listening to me.

"I have to go to LA tomorrow. *Mi madre.*"

Dread focused my attention. "Is she hurt?"

"She's not so well," was all he'd admit.

Thinking cancer, then heart failure, I wanted to cry. Headache was still after Tomás. What had I done?

"I fly out of Boston tomorrow night," he said.

"I'll drive you," I said. It was the least I could do.

"That's a very bad idea."

"Why? It's been safe, even without Rayna—"

"Stay in town!"

I felt so sorry for him, and now he was losing his mom, probably because of me. "Then I'll take you to the bus," I said. "It's only twenty minutes on the interstate."

"Lee, I don't know, it'll be dark."

I wasn't sure what difference dark made, and I was sure I owed Tomás this ride. "Tomás, please let me help you get to your mom. The Voice will keep me safe." I wasn't entirely sure about the last part, but it seemed persuasive.

A brilliant sunset was turning dull gray when we got on the interstate the next evening. Tomás gazed out his window, apparently trapped in his thoughts. I, on the other hand, felt confident and strong.

"How are you doing?" I asked.

He motioned that he didn't want to talk.

To reassure him, I said, "I promise, all of this is going to get resolved,"

"You can't resolve this. I'm in an argument with God."

This was hardly progress, to blame God instead of himself. I was about to tell him so when he interrupted. "Where's your phone?"

Fishing it from my pocket, I passed it to him. He entered some text and gave it back. "I put Janice in your contacts. Her name is Warren."

I pocketed the phone. "Tomás, God's not responsible for this pain. This is Headache."

He threw a dark look in my direction. "Now you're the expert on God?"

"No," I replied with dignity, "but I know Headache."

We didn't speak after that. It was too cold to stand outside, so we waited in the car for the bus, Tomás turning his internet ticket over and over. When the bus pulled in, we crossed the street and I stood behind him as they stowed his bag in the baggage compartment. Before he could turn toward the steps, I threw my arms around him and hugged him as hard as I could. He made a sound, which could have been a single sob, pulled away, and boarded without looking back.

Returning to my car, I felt oddly dislocated. When I put the key in the ignition, I realized I'd forgotten to wish his mom and family comfort and peace. This failure was too much to bear and, sitting in my car on this well lit street, I broke down crying. Once started, it was impossible to stop and I became afraid some kind soul would knock on my window to ask what the trouble was. Straining to see through my tears and trying to hold the wheel steady, I pulled out from the curb into evening traffic. A few blocks later, when I realized driving was a terrible idea, I veered into the entrance of a supermarket parking lot.

Finding a space in a corner with hedges, I turned the car off and locked the doors. Then I let myself descend into true hysteria, crying so desperately it was difficult to breathe. All my griefs merged: Tomás collapsing beside his mother's grave, Rayna's stiff body on the side of the road, Darnell dead by suicide, Bill's pitiful open mouth. I sobbed for all the wrongs I'd done my children, the injustice of my father's faraway death, the misery of orphans searching through bombed-out houses. I saw the stars in NGC 300 go out, darkness creeping through the luminous pinwheel arms. And when there was nothing left to cry about, I sat still, entirely empty and without purpose.

———

Hunger roused me. I remembered the way to the interstate, and from there to the cottage, so I backed out of my corner and left the parking lot. It seemed to be late at night and the traffic was light. I couldn't think why I'd come to the bus station. Did my family take the bus back to Boston? No, they drove up in a van. Maybe it had something to do with finding Rayna. I supposed I'd remember once I got home and had something to eat.

Approaching the interstate I was confused whether to go north or south, and instinct took me north. At first I drove in the slow lane, but it seemed I ought to be closer to the median strip. The night was so black, behind me cars were simply headlights, and ahead only fancy patterns of brake lights. I noticed many of the big trucks had a string of golden lights along the top of their cabs. Checking my left mirror, I moved into the center lane, and suddenly remembered that I'd come down to meet Rayna. She was on a bus!

But that couldn't be right, I wasn't at the bus station anymore. Then I realized she was coming on a truck to meet me, sitting up proudly on the seat beside the driver. I quickly pulled into the fast lane and someone honked, but now I knew that I had to wait for her at the median. A long, level area was approaching, so I signaled left and angled off into the snowbank. A week of cold had shrunk the snow and the car plowed through this until it stopped. Very nice, I was well off the highway.

I got out, wrapping my scarf tight and pulling up my hood against the cold. Rayna's truck would be coming down from the north, a part of the caravan of southbound trucks that owned the highway at night. I slogged across the snowy median and waited on the southbound side as the occasional car passed. Then I saw it, traveling in the slow lane, long and tall, with its line of golden cab lights. It was beautiful and it was slowing down for me. I walked across the highway to greet the driver as it rolled to a stop. But unaccountably, I was buffeted by a wind. . . .

The side of the cab was only feet from me when the truck erupted into speed and noise, thundering past me at sixty miles an hour. I reeled back from its turbulence and sensed the rush of something behind me—a car for god's sake! Gaping at its taillights as they escaped into the dark, I understood: My perception was altered. Approaching vehicles slowed or vanished, even as they bore down on me in real time. Level with me, they burst into life and I saw them for what they were. And judging by the way they raced on, I was invisible to them.

I turned to look north. The highway had expanded to eight lanes, and in each lane were the high headlights of a truck. I knew not all of these were real, but I bet at least one of them was. Stranded among the lanes and facing the distant line of trucks, I stood petrified.

A body brushed my leg, a feeling so familiar it didn't need explanation. A smaller, blacker wolf, or maybe Rayna herself, pressed against me. Instinctively, we moved as a unit, the wolf stepping right, I glued to her side, while something huge rattled past on our left. Now she pushed me to move left, I obeyed, and we held our breaths as roaring turbulence passed us first on the right, and seconds later, on the left. Together, we inched back and forth across the highway, threading our way between the real and phantom traffic. My mind shrieked, Look up! Look up! Look what's coming! But I kept my eyes locked on the wolf and let the shaking and pounding fly past us.

Then I was stumbling into the snowbank on the center median. Daring to glance up, I saw the highway had shrunk to its normal size and carried its usual nighttime traffic. My own car was still safely parked on the far side of the median, and there was no wolf anywhere to be seen. Irrational fear that I'd lost Rayna a second time sent me running north along the median, screaming for her as if she'd really been with me.

I heard my voice crack in despair and stopped in my tracks. I was being played, I had no doubt. Disgusted by Headache, and myself, I bent my head, turned south, and walked along the southbound shoulder in the direction of my car.

The hiss of air brakes behind me spun me around. A large semi barreled down the road, its trailer locked in a fishtail. My brain perceived each millisecond, passing with excruciating slowness. The long trailer body swung slowly away from me, the big front tires skidding slowly toward me. The driver's jaw was clenched as he fought in slow motion to haul his front wheels into the skid. The trailer reached the apex of its oscillation, paused for a moment and reversed, now creeping toward me in an arc that would grind me under the rear tires.

I could only watch. The driver strained at the steering wheel, the front wheels inched toward straight, the bulk of the trailer loomed larger, and the maddening front tires spun on the asphalt. Then the tires gripped, and ever so slowly the cab began to pull forward. The rear tires came slowly into line, and like a moving mountain, the whole tractor-trailer glided past me, coming to a stop some ways down the shoulder. I staggered backwards, lost my balance, and fell on my back in the snow. From there I could see how brightly the stars shone.

By the time the driver came running to me, I was sitting up, because it was vital to show him I was unhurt. I owed him everything. He was scared out of his wits, as I was, and I made no attempt to speak. Putting a heavy hand on my shoulder to steady himself, but more likely to confirm I was alive, he bent over me.

"Oh shit," he finally said.

He straightened painfully, then squatted down to look me in the face. "Jesus, what were you doing? You just took five years off my life."

I nodded sadly and handed him my cell phone, with Janice's

contact information lit up on its face, exactly as Tomás had entered it. The driver stared dumbly at the phone for a moment, then collected his wits and pressed call. I wasn't surprised when nothing happened, Headache was having quite a night of it. Shrugging, he leaned on me to stand up, sighed deeply, and trudged back to his cab with my phone. Headache might be trying to kill me, but the Voice had found me the best driver ever.

The driver returned wearing a heavy jacket and carrying a blanket and a flashlight as big as a club. I sat on the blanket while he went up the highway to look for black ice, returning to report he didn't see nothing to cause a spin out.

"Guess I lost it when you popped up in my lights." Lowering himself to the blanket, he eyed me accusingly. "Black coat with no reflectors. Are you crazy?"

He was right about the crazy, but for a different reason. Flashes of forest sunlight brightened the edges of my vision. I wanted to tell him I was having a nervous breakdown, but speech was as remote as Mars, so I just nodded mutely.

By now, he'd grasped that the lady in the black coat wasn't all there, so he shoved my cell into my pocket and busied himself with his. I was slipping in and out of the forest world and had an unreasonable urge to curl up next to him and go to sleep. The big gray wolf paced on the trail, waiting until I was ready to join her. I was nearly asleep where I sat, when Janice's car coasted past us and stopped.

Janice and a man who was surely her husband ran up. My driver jumped to his feet and took the husband aside, no doubt to tell the story of the near death of the crazy lady.

Janice leaned over me. "Lee, are you all right, hon?"

I shook my head no, but stood up anyway. We found my car keys in my pocket, and Janice's husband went across the median to drive my car back to the cottage.

My truck driver was more than ready to hand me off. "Take care of her now," he told Janice, and giving me a light punch on the arm, declared, "Lucky girl!" Then he strode back to his cab, a hero.

Once in Janice's car, I discovered access to simple sentences and managed to persuade her that what I really needed was sleep. Back at the cottage, her husband had put my car in the driveway, and he waited in her car while she saw me inside. After I demonstrated I could take butter out of the fridge and spread it on a piece of bread, she reluctantly left me. As soon as her car was gone, I abandoned the bread, lay down on the living room couch, and fell instantly asleep.

Hunting

I was immediately in the world of the wolf, watching her run through the forest and hearing the snow crackle under her paws. We were back at the beginning of the first wolf dream, and the dream moved quickly as it followed the pictures I'd left scattered on the dining room table. But this dream felt as real as actual experience because of its vast detail, which included my memories, thoughts, and feelings.

My dreaming mind knew that the person who was me lay on a couch in a little house on the coast of Maine. I also knew that the dream was a representation of the conflict between Headache and the Voice, and allowed me to join forces with the Voice. The dream was a translation from a realm of incomprehensible energies, designed for my human comprehension. Even so, I understood the consequences of my dream actions would be real.

I entered the dream willingly, because Rayna was missing and people were dead, dying, or suffering. The generous part of me had made a promise in August, and now was the time to fulfill it.

The gray wolf was built for distance and went quickly up the slope, over the ridge, and down into the valley. As she descended through the ash trees that shaded the bright June sun, her color darkened and her body shrank, until she became the little black wolf of the highway. Watching her track the prey's scent, I could see how much she looked like Rayna.

She went past the place where I'd been startled by the sound of rustling leaves inside the cottage, and we were in new territory. Now I was very apprehensive, because I was afraid of what Headache might do. If the Voice lost the conflict, were there greater horrors in store? Would this dream be the end of my sanity?

The little wolf followed the scent through a forest of pine and oak, until she reached a stream that flowed over broad granite ledges. I knew these streams from summers when my kids were little, and I relaxed. The kids would sit on squares of linoleum to slide over the wet rocks, tipping into each cascade and moving on like a cork.

Losing the scent at the water, the little black wolf circled between the forest and the stream, before pausing to drink from a shaded pool with sand at its bottom. She raised her wet nose to search the air, pointing her head in several directions, but apparently found nothing. So she began to track downstream among the scrub oaks growing at the edge of the forest, and at one point waded to the center of the stream to paw the bottom. Dissatisfied there, she came back to the bushes along the edge, and in a short time crossed the stream to work her way back up the other side.

She had no better luck there, and when she'd gone beyond where she had come out of the forest, she jumped lightly across the stream and returned to the last good scent at the edge of the forest. Here she lay down on the rocky ledge beside the pool where she'd drunk, and closed her eyes.

I heard a gust of wind rattling the leaves above me, and opened my eyes on a world without red or green. The bushes and trees around me were various shades of white, yellow, and gray. The sky was a pale, unnatural blue. The sunny rock I lay on was as dark as fresh mud.

My front vision was more narrow, but my peripheral vision extended beyond my ears. What was most astonishing was the sight of water over rocks, a sparkle of movement more wonderful than anything I'd ever seen. Stretching out a paw, I rose to investigate.

I knew these black paws I stood on. I knew these strong front legs, not the legs of a wolf but the legs of a dog. I felt my tail thrashing with excitement and realized Rayna recognized me. Or rather, recognized my presence, because the physical me was definitely not there.

I sat down on the rock, that is, Rayna sat. My human mind stalled and halted. Then it exploded with joy: Rayna, alive, with me! Completely and utterly with me, closer than was possible. We spun around and around on the rock in mutual delight.

Smells swamped my brain, the wet sand at the bottom of the

pool, rocks warmed by sun, acid forest soil, and untold lesser smells floating on the breeze. I could recognize the last good scent behind me, a delicious tang of copper and salt mixing with the foul odor of prey. Rayna knew the prey smell, it had filled the house the morning she ran away.

We ran to that scent, a patch of skin and blood, and flopped down on top of it. Our legs needling the air, we rolled our back on it until the scent was thoroughly mashed into our fur. Leaping to our feet, we shook ourself, casting the scent in a wide circle of particles that settled lightly to the ground around us.

Now I understood the wolf dream, the dream I mistook for useless allegory. The gray wolf was both Rayna and me, and together we would track and destroy Headache to free the Voice. Rayna had the nose for tracking and teeth for killing, while I had the intellect to guide our actions. It was possible the Voice had devised this plan from the beginning, and this gave me a huge feeling of confidence.

Trotting across the stream, we broadened our search until we caught the prey smell at a stand of saplings. The prey had run through the stream, making its scent damp and easy to track. Our world of smell was almost limitless, but our visual world was much smaller than I was used to. We could see detail to roughly twenty feet around us and our eye level was two feet high, but when Rayna glanced toward distant trees, I was amazed at how far away we could see the flutter of their leaves.

Coming to an open valley, a flick of movement at the other side launched Rayna into a gallop. Her big chest pumping air and black legs racing, she ran, because running down prey was what she was made for. The prey scent wafted off the top of the grass, pulling us toward a distant woods. When we entered it, the silence under the trees told us the prey had escaped.

So the chase had begun. I was aware of many levels of meaning. For Rayna, there was the canine ecstasy of running, electrified by the possibility of a kill. For me, there was the urgency of catching the prey and saving the Voice. There was also the outrage I felt toward Headache and all the suffering he caused. Beyond all this, I sensed events sweeping us toward—well, I didn't know what.

By dark, we were crossing blue-gray plains under a sky full of light. We could see well enough at night with canine vision, but the scent had dried and more and more we ran in circles to find it. So we crawled under the branches of a thicket and dug a shallow hole. Circling once, Rayna dropped into the hole and quickly fell into a light sleep, from which she would occasionally wake at a sound. She would listen for a moment to identify its cause, and reassured, sink back to sleep. All the while, I rested in the comfort of her breathing.

At dawn, light brightened outside the thicket and we smelled small animals moving in the brush. Crawling out of our den, we easily located the scent of prey in the heavy dew. To me, it stank of hate and fear.

Time did not exist for us. Instead the day's progress was marked by patterns of light. By midday, we came into a manicured landscape where trees as straight as pencils marched up the sides of steep hills. Our prey had run at a level across the slope, so we made good time over ground that was surprisingly free of underbrush. The tops of the trees were indistinct, but I knew it was high foliage that shut out the yellow sun. Gradually the trees thinned and the light increased, until we came out in the bright light of a valley crowded with pale broad-leafed bushes. They were just tall enough for a Kai to run beneath, and the ground beneath them crackled with dried leaves as we ran.

On the other side of the valley the running was harder. We were in a disorderly forest of spindly trees, with fallen trees lying at unexpected angles that made us dodge the ends of broken branches. Something large had stormed through here, smashing through dead wood as it went.

Abruptly, the land rose sharply at forty-five degrees, tough going for a human but not for a canine with a low center of gravity and four agile legs. Rayna climbed so rapidly, it was obvious this was her terrain, and I wondered if we were in the ring of Japanese mountains where her breed was born. When we stopped to pick up the scent, we heard a formless sound, perhaps a bump or a stumble, from further up the hill. Carried with the sound was the foul whiff of our enemy. Rayna sprang forward and we flowed up the mountainside in a series of quick switchbacks, like a river running uphill.

The slope leveled off into a clearing of tall, hollow grasses. Beyond the clearing something large was rushing away through the underbrush. Rayna locked on this with absolute focus and we tore after it. Her excitement was intense but without anger. I, on the other hand, wanted vengeance.

The advantage of our small size was speed, and as we closed on the running shape, we raised an intimidating barrage of barks. I couldn't make out the big creature that fled from us and dreaded to see the physical form Headache would take. From this distance, it was only a large bulk crashing through the trees.

We entered a second clearing, where the grasses stood quietly, in anticipation. The smell of prey was thick and Rayna danced in place, while I was merely puzzled. All of a sudden, the prey burst out of the underbrush, heading straight for us. It was covered by bristles, humpbacked, round like a barrel, and four times our size. Little dark eyes glared above large tusks that curved lethally outward.

We leapt out of the way and let the wild boar dash past, a hundred and fifty pounds to our thirty-five. For such a big creature it moved fast, but I was able to see its tusks clearly. I couldn't possibly let my dear, flesh and blood companion get near those razor edges. Rayna reared up on hind legs and raked the air with our paws, held back by the force of my fear. We dropped down and whirled in a tight circle.

Release her! She is not afraid! the Voice commanded in a hard masculine tone.

Of course, I obeyed. I gave myself to Rayna's instincts and let her go.

We shot after the boar, a missile with teeth and claws. Flying past trees and through brush, we gained on it quickly. With the big haunches right in front of us, we avoided its hooves and sprang at the hind quarters, teeth ripping skin and tongue tasting blood. The boar spun on us, but we darted out of range, and now waited at a distance, trembling with excitement. Uncertain of the thing that attacked him, and possibly because we were downwind and motionless, the boar seemed to forget us and walked away.

Rayna had no doubt this was the creature that had tried to kill her and hurt me. Besides, she'd tasted its blood and her prey drive was fully ignited. Her muscles tensed, we raced in to snap at his flank, and this time the boar understood the danger. Turning fast, he lowered his head to fight. We barked in his face, bouncing up and down and thrashing our tail, to make ourself an intimidating opponent. Kai are not big dogs, so their job is to bring the game to bay while they summon the hunter with their raucous barking. For something as big as this boar, Kai hunted in twos or threes.

The hog went stiff-legged and popped his jaws to sharpen his tusks, slobber foaming over his lips. Instinctively, Rayna knew this was a deadly stance. Staring at the boar's dripping mouth and small black eyes, I saw Headache's fury. Who is the hunter, I thought, and when is he coming?

The big pig lunged at us again and we jumped back to safety. I could tell this was going to be a contest of patience and stamina, an effort to wear the other down. The boar had power and courage, we had speed and agility, and I didn't see an advantage on either side. I knew Rayna would rely on me to finish the boar off, but I realized that I had no idea how to get it done.

We ducked back into the brush so the boar would lose track of us, then jumped him from behind, flinging ourself at his less protected hips. His big body twisted to face us just as we vanished into the tall grass. Coming at him from a new angle, we ripped at his back leg and escaped once more. Rayna could probably keep this up indefinitely, but what if I lost my focus? What if the boar had his own store of inexhaustible energy? I wasn't at all sure I could keep going.

But, I realized, I should be. This wasn't new, it was something I'd been doing for years: pushing through the swim and gaining strength as my body loosened up; settling into the bike to pace myself over the distance; and running full out, where only my breathing counted. So many triathlons had trained me for this sustained effort, and I knew what I was doing. This dream played to my strengths, and the Voice must have arranged it that way.

I let Rayna dodge and dart, while I considered how to bring the boar down. We lacked a weapon, but we had climbed a steep slope to get here. In my imagination I saw a rocky gorge, a wild and slippery place. If the boar rolled down it, would he be stunned or killed? I'd have to leave that part up to the Voice.

We were chasing and dodging in a level clearing, which meant we needed to get the boar to the downward slope, wherever that was. Perhaps Rayna could smell it. I fixed my mind on a dangerous slope, and I believe Rayna grasped the plan. She began to jump in the boar's face to infuriate him. He sharpened his tusks, dropped his head, and charged. With a burst of elation, Rayna sprang up over his head, spun half-way around in the air above him, and landed behind him, facing his rear. We could see him stop and sway, unsure where we had gone.

Then we fell relentlessly on his hindquarters and he fled. Pursuing him through a grove of large, multi-trunked trees, I saw how the land fell away to the side, exposing the tops of trees below us. Under the racket of our barking we could hear the rush of water.

We turned him down this slope and pursued him deeper into the woods. The water grew louder and the forest darker, as we descended. An ancient landslide had created a steep gorge of fallen rocks, where a fast moving stream raced down the mountainside from one waterfall to the next. Laurel branches twisted in bizarre shapes over the sharp-edged rocks, as if the gorge was haunted. At the bottom of the falls thirty feet below, the force of pouring water had cut a deep channel that rushed away under the laurel branches and disappeared around a bend.

Pushing the pig hard toward the gorge, we sprang at his haunches over and over, pulling out bristles and biting flesh. I felt his fright and lost all restraint, impatient to tear him apart.

He made a stand at the top of the gorge, backing into the water that rushed over the first waterfall. In my frenzy, we took a wild chance and jumped for his ear. His huge head snapped up, his hooves slipped on wet rock and he went down on his side. In a moment the water pulled him over the edge and the big body dropped, bounced, and slid from one rock surface to the next. Racing down through the forest, we kept pace with his rough descent. At the bottom falls, he tumbled off the rock and splashed into the deep channel. We leapt across the channel in time to see him, head up, being carried around the bend. It looked like he might be swimming.

Inside the racket of the water, it was very still. Now I could feel a bright gash of pain burning across our thigh, and we sank back on the wet moss. There was a strong smell of blood and when we raised our head, we could see a dark gray liquid oozing from a wound that crossed our thigh. With an effort, we delicately licked the wound, and laid our head back down on the rock. Later, when we noticed our thirst, we rose painfully to limp to the stream, and drank as long as we could. Then we gazed around us, searching for a shelter to hide in. There was a small concave area in the jumble of rocks above us. Slowly we climbed to it and lay down to wait until we could walk. Rayna had no foresight and didn't question whether we would walk again, but I did.

Dark daylight shifted to evening blue. We rolled onto our elbows to lick the wound and lay back with a sigh. Rayna slipped into a hot sleep, while I suffered remorse for both of us. I guessed we wouldn't be able to move in the morning, that fever and pain would keep us here until we were too weak to stand and thirst shut down our organs. It was more or less how Bill died.

Was this how goodness would survive in the cosmos, the boar swept away and Rayna and I dying quietly beside a waterfall? It made cosmic sense that this was our end, clean, unsentimental, and highly suitable for non-believers. I would have liked the certainty of freeing the Voice, a proclamation or a beautiful sunset, but I could make my peace with laurel bushes and the sound of falling water. After all, I was dying with my best companion.

But wait. What if I didn't die? There was no guarantee I would die with her. The thought that I would survive her was almost unbearable—I ought to be the one to die, because it was my fault she was cut. When we jumped into the boar's face, he flicked his head and grazed her thigh with his tusk. If she died and I didn't, I would live out my life without her, knowing that I'd killed her. I cried out in anguish and heard Rayna utter a long canine wail in her sleep.

It is not yet done, the Voice said softly.

I sensed brightness, as if the moon had just cleared the trees, but

Rayna's eyes were shut and I could see nothing. Kindness wrapped us like mist and it occurred to me it was possible to forgive myself for Rayna's death.

Losing contact with the pain in our thigh, the solid rock, and the sound of water, the gates that guarded my perception opened. Rayna's body twitched as I left it.

I was immersed in a profusion of conscious life, swirling and boiling with so many creatures I could barely grasp the immensity of it. Very few were human, all had awareness, some had wants. It might have been how the Voice experienced life, and it went on and on, expanding my awareness.

At times, humans emerged from the froth and became recognizable to me because I loved them. At the 10K finish line Bill emptied a water bottle over his head and hopped around like a fool. I hadn't met him yet, but he told me about it later. He said it was the happiest moment of his life.

On opposite sides of the bassinet, Susan and Cara stood rapt with wonder. The baby stared solemnly at his sisters from the folds of his blanket. Cara reached in and opened a little balled hand. "Watch this," she told Susan, touching the baby's palm. His little fingers fastened around her index finger in a death grip.

The older Latina was propped up by pillows so she could breathe more easily. Her face and abdomen were swollen, and so were the legs that moved restlessly under the covers. Tomás, his older sister and his brother, stood around the bed, while their father clung to the mother's hand and wept. She had the bad luck to be dying before her husband and couldn't bring herself to leave him bereft. In a day, she would give up the urgency of life and begin to commune with the visions that gathered in the room. Hearing her murmur the names of dead family members would comfort her husband.

But now was the hard time. Usually her eyes were closed, her mouth open, and seconds would pass between one breath and the next. Sometimes she cried, "oh, oh!" and her children would flinch because they thought she was in pain. Her daughter wiped away bubbles at the corner of her mouth and Tomás dropped to his knees beside the bed. He prayed for her release, but more than that, he preyed that God would forgive his anger. For the child who had given his life to keep the family safe, this death was a terrible broken promise.

One by one, the people I loved vanished back into the swirl of animal consciousness. Now my attention picked up the whispering energy of the plants growing on the mountains where Rayna slept, and from that to the interwoven energy of all plants on the surface of the Earth. Below this was a deeper, slower energy, the enduring consciousness of the Earth's minerals and rocks. And beyond all of that, I detected the faint conscious hum of particles that constituted the building blocks of matter. Stunned and thrilled, my awareness swept out to the physical universe.

I could feel the oxygen molecules bound in the air above the Earth, and the atoms and subatomic particles that made them up. I noticed how the planet's atmosphere thinned quickly to the vacuum of space, and how the rotating Earth composed itself in layers, from its hot solid core to the magma of its mantle and its egg-shell thin crust of rock. I marveled at what a tiny pebble the Earth was, and at how great a distance it orbited its sun. Soon I could detect the pin pricks where the other planets traveled a solar system of seven billion miles.

Beyond the planets, this sun was only one of the thousands of stars in a spiral arm of a galaxy. I located this galaxy at the edge of a cluster of a thousand galaxies, and when I let my mind expand, I saw how the cluster fit into an immense supercluster of one hundred thousand galaxies covering more than five hundred million light years. Holding all of this in motion as it traversed the vast regions where dark matter hid, was the dip and curve of gravity.

I wanted to reach out to the other ten million superclusters in the observable universe, but the Voice interrupted.

Return to your world. You belong with your spirit.

Abruptly I was back in Rayna's body, feeling her fast heartbeats and the heat of her fever.

Is she dying? I asked the Voice. Because if she dies, I'd rather stay with the galaxies.

The dream is not done.

I don't understand you.

Your spirit must live until the dream is done.

So she'll recover?

I am allowed to help her.

"Allowed" seemed like an odd word for a cosmic being, but I waited.

It is because you protected me. Greater beings operate within frameworks. One of these is reciprocity.

If they had frameworks, why did they need to fight?

Headache and I are opposing energies. We do not fight.

It looks like fighting to me.

Headache and I are antagonistic. Our struggle is one current among many in the universe.

I absorbed this, and she continued.

Understand there is no "I" and no "Headache." These names are how we translate our existence for you.

I understand.

We are energetic. Within this dream what you and your spirit do is energetic. That is how you play your part.

That was clear enough to me, as far as it went.

You are right that Headache wants to annihilate me. I am kinder than Headache and do not need to destroy him. But he fears me. His intent is to destroy me.

What happens if he does?

Certain aspects of being are no longer available.

A wave of darkness blotting out the stars?

Yes. Or a sudden loss of everything you love. You have premonitions of this.

Remembering the beach, I became anxious. Will it last forever? I asked her.

Headache and I exist in an eternal present. Neither of us knows our end.

But you must know. I saw a baby that hasn't been born yet.

There are many possible futures and the baby is just one of them.

Then what's the point of the struggle with Headache?

Energy follows its course and arrives at an outcome. You and your spirit and I do what we can.

That's not very enlightening, I thought, and felt a jolt.

Listen carefully. You and your spirit are not bound by our frameworks. We do not know your role. You are unpredictable elements.

I asked uneasily, What does that mean?

You have great power.

I was ok with the hum of elemental particles, the layers of the Earth and its distance to the sun, and even with a galaxy supercluster spanning five hundred million light years. None of that had anything to do with me. I was not ok with having great power, which was ridiculous. For a while I listened to Rayna breathing.

Why did you pick me? I finally asked.

I did not pick you. You wandered into a place where you were not expected.

The night had gotten cooler. Rayna opened her eyes and I saw gleaming water whirling downhill. Our pain had drifted into the dark, the fever was gone with the mist. We stretched out our front and back paws as far as we could, and got comfortable.

Echoes of Mercy

At dawn the next morning we came down from our cave to drink from the stream. As we lifted our nose from the water, the smell of wolf made us look up. On the high bank of the wooded side of the gorge, a large gray wolf stood watching us. She was more powerful than the wolf in my drawings and I was ecstatic—the real hunter had come at last! I guessed she embodied the Voice just as the boar embodied Headache, maintaining the symmetry of their antagonism. She whirled away into the forest and we jumped the stream, bounding up the rocks to follow her through the trees.

She led us down past the bend in the channel where the boar had disappeared. There we split up to track on either side of the stream, looking for the place where he came onto land. Rayna and the wolf shared the kinship of canids, immersed in the present and its movement and smells. With the wolf hunting beside us I felt childishly happy, and imagined the two of them hanging out together during Christmas.

As the slope pitched downwards, the stream poured over huge boulders, stacked haphazardly on top of each other by whatever landslide had tumbled them. The boar must have fallen and bounced from rock to rock as the water pushed him along. He was at least one night ahead of us, and I wondered whether he would hide beside the stream, waiting until we passed to charge us from behind. A boar wouldn't be cunning enough to do that, although Headache certainly was. But so far the dream had adhered to expected animal behavior, which was probably another of those frameworks the greater beings followed. It was a good thing reliable principles governed here, but then, the physical universe had always been reliable.

For someone who'd never believed in God, it was strange how I

believed in the Voice. My natural pessimism had tipped over into optimism, and it didn't seem possible we'd fail. Wasn't goodness more
powerful than suffering, regardless of what I used to think about the
injustice of the world? It had occurred to me that harboring the Voice
in my brain might have altered my thinking, creating the devotion
Tomás saw in me. When this contest was done, I could return to
thinking whatever I wanted.

As the mountainside flattened into the surrounding land, the
stream spread into a shallow river that gurgled between scattered boulders. Keeping the wolf in sight as we worked the opposite bank, Rayna
and I knew immediately when her head jerked up and she sprang
forward. Leaping from rock to rock, we caught up with her as she
sniffed a large ring of grass, flattened around a crater of mud and
sand. The pig had wallowed there the night before, leaving the smells
of urine, feces, and blood.

At a dead run, we chased his scent from the river and out onto
flat grassland, where lush white grass extended for miles before us.
He'd left a wide track through the grass, a boulevard to his intended
destination. Clearly, he wanted us to follow. We passed no buildings
or barns, but did find a drainage ditch, where we drank and lay down
to rest. Then we were up and in pursuit once more. Boars were fast,
but we were faster.

By afternoon, the soil had become drier, the grass shorter and
grayer. I noticed a black line along the horizon, which grew until it
was a thick black band, and then a black cloud filling half the sky. The
wind picked up, blowing a faint smell of prey into our faces, as the
cloud turned midnight black and began to spit flashes of lightning. In
Rayna's canine vision, violent bolts of neon appeared to freeze in the
air as they shot from cloud to cloud or cloud to earth. I hated this wild
energy, tearing the air with its force. Was it a warning from Headache
that he would triumph? Tomás had said that evil spirits didn't bring
the weather.

The storm did not discourage the canids, who squinted into the
pelting rain to keep the boar's form in sight. The wolf sprinted full out
and had the speed to overtake him, when all at once the storm passed
overhead and the prairie lit up with sun.

We slowed. The boar had disappeared in the sunlight, but then, so had the prairie. Now we trotted over arid, sandy soil that was covered by patches of wiry, gray grass. The air was thin and hot, and occasionally we passed a mass of pale rock that folded over itself like stiff pudding. In the distance I could see low, blue shapes that extended across the land for miles, reminding me of something that made me uneasy.

Still on the boar's trail, we now ran on sand and fragments of shale, at the beginning of what must be a great desert. Far from us, I could make out massive formations with flat tops, and wide rock skirts that anchored them to the earth. I knew these were mesas, and their cap rocks stood a thousand feet above the desert floor. It was the place of my falling nightmare, and the boar was leading us straight to it. That's when my fantasy of success came apart. I realized the Voice was no longer in charge of the dream, and probably never had been.

Approaching a huge mesa, the big wolf jumped onto its skirts, and we had to slow down to negotiate the loose rock and broken shale. Dry as the air was, the boar's scent was clear and took us onto a trail that snaked up the side of the mesa. We climbed quickly, our paws getting good purchase on the rough sandstone. He must be close ahead, because we saw his footprints in the red dust and smelled his stink and anger.

Reaching the rimrock, we jumped onto the flat top of the mesa. There were grasses here, desert shrubs, and absolutely no place to hide. The sun was down in the west, casting long shadows of bushes in our direction. At its western edge, the mesa ended in some fashion that canid vision couldn't make out, but that canid smell completely understood. I struggled to put aside my terror, so it wouldn't get in Rayna's way. Trust in the wolf, I repeated in my thoughts, trust her.

The boar stood thirty feet from us, ready to charge as soon as we moved in from the rim. Neither the wolf nor Rayna had any fear, for their prey was right before them, wrapped in the intoxicating smells of blood and anger. The wolf stepped carefully, using her cunning to assess the boar's stance and power. Rayna knew this enemy all too well, and waited for a twitch of the wolf's ear to begin the attack.

He chose to hurl himself at us with remarkable speed. Rayna

spun out from under his tusks, cutting in the opposite direction, as the wolf jumped him from behind and sank her teeth into his back. I thought she would bring him down with one bite, but he braced his feet and shook her off, foam flying from his tusks.

As an animal, the boar was tough and courageous, but when Rayna and I challenged him eye to eye, rage boiled off him in waves. Looking into those fierce eyes, I saw only Headache and my own rage exploded. Rayna reacted by flinging ourself at his face and we barely escaped.

With awful clarity, I realized she was ready to die for me. But she had no concept that I was in her body and would die with her. Our blissful union had a tragic liability: I couldn't call her to me and she couldn't see that I was safe.

This wasn't the struggle I'd wanted, it wasn't a fight for right and goodness where the Voice triumphs. It was a confused and horrifying jumble, like most fights probably were. I had no power to help the Voice or Rayna. I could not erase the mesa's fearful edge. I had no part in the vast energies that surrounded us, energies that locked up, broke apart, tangled, and twisted. And whether I wanted it or not, the energies were moving this mess toward a conclusion.

The three animals crisscrossed the open top of the mesa, and no one had the advantage. The boar was the biggest and most dangerous, with his razor tusks. The wolf was powerful and quick, and could run circles around the boar. Rayna was the fastest and most agile, darting in and out to distract the boar from attacking the wolf. Together the wolf and Rayna might defeat the boar, but only, I thought, if they were lucky.

Once more the wolf jumped at boar's haunches. This time her bite broke the skin and she worked to get her jaws on his spine. Was this cruelty, or just a translation of antagonism? What was I supposed to do? I withdrew my mind from the melee, despairing that this fight could ever be made right.

The sun was on the horizon. The wolf was grimly gnawing through the boar's backbone to cripple him. Dragging his useless back feet, he moved slowly toward the edge of the mesa, hauling the wolf with him. He intended to roll her over the edge, while she tried to wound him mortally before he got that far. Rayna raced around them, dashing in to bite the boar's legs but unable to stop his progress.

We were feet away from the edge. I could feel the lift of air from the canyon floor. The boar was staggering and ready to fall. The wolf had clamped her teeth on his backbone but still he moved. I was certain there was nothing I could do.

From the energy surrounding me came a shove, pushing me awake. Rayna and I were one, devoted to each other. The Voice counted on us both. I came to life, and together Rayna and I jumped at the boar to save the Voice.

We threw ourself into the boar's face and he butted us with his massive head. In the same moment, the wolf leaped to protect us, seizing the boar's ear and bringing him to the ground. The boar thrashed his huge body, trying to fling the wolf off, Rayna and I were swept to the edge, and all three animals went over together.

I remember every second of that terrible fall. It went on forever, no grace, no courage, no epiphany, just accelerating fear. I knew I'd feel my body shatter when we hit, and I did. We hit with a force that blew Rayna and me apart.

———

How do you survive a fall like that? I blacked out, came to, blacked out again. Always in the background was a small, disturbing cough.

The burden of the cough became greater and greater, until I had to attend to it. I woke up on cool desert sand and managed to raise my head, trying to locate the source of the cough. Rayna lay on her side a few feet from me, struggling to breathe. I squirmed through the sand, close enough that I could slip my arms around her, and saw how her ribs had caved in from the blow of the boar's head. That's when I realized that I'd need more courage now than I'd ever need again. Holding her in my arms and looking firmly into her eyes, I watched their brightness die and her breathing stop.

The sun had set behind the canyon and it was full dark down on the desert. The Milky Way was so dense with stars that it lit the ground, making the sand around me white as a beach. I held Rayna, grappling with what had just happened. She had left me, and there was a hole in my world that couldn't be explained.

The final leap in the boar's face had cost Rayna her life. But that was both our decisions, wasn't it? We jumped to save the Voice, and Rayna had always been willing to die for me. In fact, she was ready to die for me from the morning Headache attacked me at the beach, and he knew it. He feared her most of all. Could he foresee she would kill him? Because surely he died in the fall.

Although, did he? I had survived, and a greater being should have more chance of surviving than me. What if Rayna was only an insignificant casualty, an expendable pet. No, it couldn't be, Rayna was my spirit! The Voice was the energy of goodness, she wouldn't let Rayna die for nothing. But she wasn't a god, able to command who died and who didn't. If I understood the greater beings at all, it was that they fit a larger purpose.

The sound of a sigh alerted me that there was more to come. Laying Rayna down on the sand, I staggered to my feet. Behind me was a broad stone, on which lay a form that glowed in the starlight. It looked alarmingly like a woman's body.

Stumbling to the rock, I sank down beside it. She was truly as beautiful as the moon and this close she shimmered with tiny ripples of light. Her eyes were open, but it was clear to me the fall had shattered her spine. The only movement left to her was a small twitch of her fingers.

I cautiously put a hand on her arm and felt how warm she was. Becoming braver, I took her hand in both of mine and held it. I searched her face for pain, but her expression was impassive, neither suffering nor serene. This was someone, or something, I loved, a precious being I wanted to save, and I was powerless.

Her form began to drift between genders, her body becoming more and more transparent. But this was impossible, Rayna had died for her! What kind of horrible universe did we live in? My fingers and arms tingled with energy until her body vanished from the stone and I held nothing.

Mashing my face into the stone, I howled without sound. Voiceless. I hit the rock with my fists until my hands hurt and I had to stop. Turning at last to face the desert, I put my back against the rock and looked into the sky. High in the Milky Way, at random and one by one, stars were blinking out. In the profound silence of the desert, I could hear the little pinging sounds of their death, like water drops on metal.

I stared at the stars. A whole region of the cosmos, abandoned by goodness, ruled by suffering. It didn't feel possible. But wasn't that how I used to imagine life was, a struggle against injustice and suffering? Except for Rayna, who I allowed to bring true happiness into my life. Now she was gone and I was back in an unjust world.

The odor of shit, vomit, and blood brought my attention down to the desert, where a dark red glow lurched across the sand. Oh yes, the winner would have to make an appearance! The glow moved in fitful jerks and I let him come, feeling increasing excitement. I could still play a role in the contest between Headache and the Voice.

He was in human form, dragging himself on his belly by the strength of his arms. Slobber ran down his chest, an open wound was on his back, and the tatters of his legs trailed him like bloody streamers. They must have been wrecked by our teeth, or his fall to the desert.

Stopping some feet away, he surveyed the empty rock with eyes the color of arterial blood.

I am too late. I wanted to eat her human flesh before she disappeared.

Why did this despicable thing survive, when the good ones died? So I could kill him, obviously.

He smiled at me, a peculiar distortion of the mouth. I could see how killing him could complete my life. To begin with, it would avenge Rayna and the Voice. It could avenge the death of Tomás' mother and old Mr. Taylor. It might even avenge the little girl who stood on her desk, sobbing while the teacher ridiculed her.

"Sit up," I ordered him. "You look like a worm. I can't talk to a worm."

He laughed and swirled in place, casting a ring of stink around himself.

"Sit up," I shouted, stepping toward him with menace. He pushed himself up on his arms until he sat in the middle of his ruined body. I wanted to kill this creature, as much as I wanted Rayna alive again.

"Well, is this it?" I jeered.

We are not done.

"Oh? Do I finally get to rip you to pieces?"

He made a sad clown face. *You cannot do that now. You killed the thing that had the teeth.*

I had to keep myself from running at him. He might grab me, and would probably try to eat me. So I held onto my hatred and began to prowl around the red circle of light at a safe distance.

"I know what I'm supposed to do," I boasted.

He grinned with satisfaction, which was even more peculiar than his smile. I wasn't frightening him, which could be because I had no way to kill him. I pivoted where I stood, looking for promising weapons. Rocks of various sizes were strewn near my feet, further away the crumbled skirt of the mesa began. Behind me was the rock where the Voice had died . . . and close to it lay Rayna's quiet body, jet black on white sand.

The shock of grief undid me. For an instant I was an empty shell, the next moment filled with fury. I grabbed up a heavy rock and threw it with a precision that astounded me. It split the side of his head, knocking him back. He rocked forward and I felt the thrill of fulfilling my purpose, but he didn't fall. Instead, he tottered on his hips until he could regain his balance and straighten himself up. The damn creature wouldn't die easily. But I could deal with that, it was an opportunity to make him suffer more.

I walked out into the desert, eager to find something that would bust his head open, and felt a hand on my arm. Turning, I saw it was Tomás, in full clerical kit. I could only gape at the mystery that had brought Tomás to witness my bloodlust.

I pulled away from him, afraid of what he was going to say, but I saw sympathy in his eyes and that gave me courage. So I flung myself on him, pressing myself as close to him as I could. He put his arms around me and there we were, standing together. I felt nourished, my heart settled, and the thing he'd called my soul came back to me. I remembered the joy Rayna had been when she was alive.

A momentary thought of Headache made me glance away from Tomás to check the desert, expecting to see that Headache had vanished in this excess of love. He had not. From inside his dark red glow his battered face glared at me. It struck me as funny that he could still be present amid all this goodness, and I looked back to share the joke with Tomás. But Tomás was gone. I was alone in the desert with the thing I hated.

I retreated to the stone where the Voice had died. It was still warm, giving the heat of the day back to the night. Leaning against it, I could feel the comfort of its warmth, and Headache was smart enough to keep his mouth shut.

I knew it wasn't Tomás who'd just held me, that Tomás was on a plane to the west coast. This Tomás was a vision, something Tomás himself would consider as real as ordinary experience. I might know the vision was unreal, but like Tomás said, it didn't really matter what I knew. The vision had stopped the violence that would have wrecked Headache, and wrecked me as well. I looked into the red glow, from which Headache watched me intently.

"What happens now that she's dead?" I demanded.

They are both dead, he said carefully. For better or worse, I did know him well. He wasn't afraid when I shattered his skull, but he was now.

"I'm talking about the greater being who died on this rock."

We do not know our future.

"But it's over. She said my spirit would live until the struggle was over, and my spirit is dead."

It is a dream.

"Don't lie," I said with disgust. "It's a translation for me, but it has real consequences."

You are deluded. You always have been.

He'd told Tomás the same thing and I wondered what he was covering up. Then I guessed it.

"We're not done. That's what you said."

His face twitched with apprehension, or whatever counted as apprehension in a being like him. No, I realized, we weren't nearly done. She'd told me, "You are unpredictable elements."

Another star died with a ping and my hands began to tremble. I looked up at the stars, promising them that when this was over I would restore their light, because the universe needed them.

He was a mess, bleeding from the shattered side of his head, his wounded back still bloody, and his legs destroyed. Somebody needs to do something about the blood, I thought, taking off the scarf I'd worn on the highway.

Up close he was even more foul than at a distance. He would have squirmed away over the sand, but something in the way I approached kept him immobile. Very carefully, I touched the scarf to the blood running down his neck. His red glow deepened, which meant his energy was sinking. Never mind how I knew this, I didn't care. I saw panic in his eyes.

There was something I needed to say to him. "I forgive you for tormenting me," I began and stopped. My words filled the air, taking on an independent existence. I thought, this is what Tomás would want me to say.

However, there was a lot more to forgive. "Listen to me," I told him. "I forgive you for setting me on fire." Did I? I supposed I did, it was the least of his sins. The look in his anxious red eyes might be pleading, although I doubted he had the capacity.

My hands shook as I cleaned off the blood behind his ear. "I forgive you for Mr. Taylor's pain and fear," I said, even though I knew the poor old man didn't deserve the death he got.

The words I was speaking were something I owed the Voice. They certainly didn't feel like my words. I looked at this creature with his pathetic back and legs, and added, "I'm sorry I hurt you. Please forgive me."

As I dabbed the blood on his back with my scarf, my arms were buzzing with some kind of tremor. Exactly why was I doing this? "I forgive you for the harm you did Darnell, and Tomás, and his mom," I continued, wanting to get this over with. And because he was the source of suffering, I forgave him all the suffering he had ever caused, and wondered how I had the power to do that. He had sunken into such a weak thing, I pitied him as much as I'd pitied anybody.

With one more thing left to say, I struggled to speak. Afraid if I said it aloud, it might become real, my whole body began to shake. Still, I spoke for the Voice and it had to be said.

"I forgive you for my Rayna's death," I told him, weeping.

The most surprising thing of all was the love I felt for this stinking, red-eyed creature.

———

Sunlight in my eyes woke me up. It came through the living room window and hit me square in the face as the sun rose. The cottage was freezing, so I got up to turn up the heat and returned to the couch. The scarf I'd had on the night before lay crumpled on the floor. I checked that it wasn't bloody, and put it around my neck thoughtfully. The hyperreal quality of the dream, so intense and layered, surrounded me. Settling my eyes on the snow outside, I began to think through the dream.

The struggle must be over or I would still be asleep, I reasoned. All the rest was complicated. Was Headache diminished and would there be less suffering in the world? Was the Voice truly gone and her energy lost? It didn't feel as though there was less goodness in the world. Actually, looking at the sunlight tinting the snow orange, it felt as if there was more.

The morning was silent and full of peace. I guessed this had to do with the sheer improbability of my forgiving Headache. Tomás put me up to it of course, or rather the vision of Tomás did. His kindness stopped me from giving Headache the outcome that Headache wanted, which was having me bash his head in. Did the Voice call the vision of Tomás with her dying energy? Did the vision come from Tomás' God? Or did Tomás have the power to turn himself into a vision? Whichever way it happened, it saved me.

I reviewed how the struggle had unfolded: Headache and the Voice were equally powerful until they went over the edge of the mesa. The fall killed the unlucky Voice but Headache survived. And there I was, some kind of loose cannon. It wasn't a simple last-man-standing kind of outcome. Headache wanted me to murder him, so that the energy of suffering would triumph. In a way I didn't understand, the dying Voice maintained the energy of goodness while Headache faded.

But had she? She vanished and I was the one who forgave Headache. The love I felt for him was genuine. I was a stand-in for the

Voice, saying her words, conveying her goodness. I even touched her and held her hand. I played her part until . . . well what, I woke up?

This wasn't a satisfying explanation. Then I remembered the weird business with the stars, how when I saw them dying, I promised them I'd bring them back to life. As if I could. What was all that about? I closed my eyes and opened my mind.

Of course. Rayna and I, unpredictable elements.

I thought of how my arms buzzed with energy when the Voice died, and how I trembled when I told Headache all the things I forgave him for. I wasn't speaking to him, her goodness was. I held the Voice's energy, not forever but certainly then. I was the improbable link who made herself available to carry the Voice's energy across . . . what, a gap? I maintained her goodness and Headache faded in the strength of it.

For a while I didn't move, my mind resting in a place without thought. Then I returned to the present and allowed myself to address the part I'd put to the side. What about Rayna, was she truly dead? It felt as though she was, although there was no physical evidence. And might never be. In the dream, Rayna's life was linked to the end of the struggle, so by dream logic she had to die. It was a dream but with real consequences, and I could only guess what these were. I found myself sitting on the couch, weeping for my last companion.

Getting up for a tissue, I saw my drawing pad in the dining room, buried under all the wolf drawings. I brought it into the kitchen, where the bread from the night before waited patiently for me. So I sat down to eat the bread, and began to draw Rayna from memory, both as a memorial to her and as a way to keep her alive. Because, after all, there are many possible futures.

The movement of my hand, and the deepening black of Rayna's face, comforted me. If the dream was in any way true, who had I become? A powerful person, if I remembered correctly. Would power make a difference in my life? Rayna was the only thing I wanted, and I doubted I had any power in that area. It was a shame. If goodness was alive in the world, you'd think one dog could make it back to me. But goodness wasn't personal, there were so many conscious creatures and so many of them had wants.

A car coasted down my driveway, my friend Janice checking up on me. She entered the kitchen cheerfully.

"Nice to see you're up! I hope you got a rest."

"I'm better than last night," I replied, my attention on the drawing.

"Let's see what you have there," she said, coming to look over my shoulder. "Oh, that's a good likeness!"

She didn't expect me to break out crying. "I'm so sorry! Did you get bad news?"

I shook my head. It felt stupid to say it was a dream, but that's what I said.

Knowing enough to let me have my grief, she sat beside me while I cried. Eventually, I got myself together and stood up. Tears spotted the drawing, making black velvet circles in the pencil shading.

"Let's go for a walk," I proposed.

Outside, I turned us down the road Rayna and I had walked last October. I'm a person of power, I thought, and I will deal with what's given to me. As we went along, I pointed out the places Rayna liked to explore. It felt better to talk about her.

"Will you get another puppy if she doesn't come back?"

"Maybe. Or maybe I'll go to California to live with my daughter. They're having another baby."

"Family's important," Janice observed, but after a bit she spoke up more enthusiastically. "When summer comes you should draw the beach and the houses. I think your pictures will do very nicely up here."

I wondered if I had a new life waiting for me, without Rayna or possibly Tomás. In some ways I guessed I was brand new, but I couldn't imagine a future without at least one of them.

Janice and I came to the field where the wild turkeys had paraded.

"Last fall Rayna saw a bunch of wild turkeys walking out there," I told her. "She jumped into the field and cut her paw on a broken bottle."

Wandering up the road to study the snowbanks, I imagined last fall's bushes frozen and brown under the snow. "I always meant to come back and pick up the glass."

Stopping, I pointed, "I think it was here."

"Lee!" Janice cried, grabbing my arm.

Across the white field, a black dog a little bigger than a fox was running toward us, fast.

Exit Point

On a windless day at the end of January, when you can just start to feel the warmth of the sun, Tomás and I sat side by side on a boulder overlooking the beach. He'd returned from LA only the week before, appearing to have more or less accepted his loss. But he looked older than I remembered and seemed distant. Grief, I assumed.

Down on the beach, Rayna was eyeing a stout brown seagull that strutted back and forth over the seaweed, as it searched for edibles. Fastening her gaze on the fat bird, Rayna sank into a crouch, head thrust forward and tail stiff. Advancing one leg at a time with infinite caution, she closed the gap between herself and the prey. When she was within striking distance and the bird hadn't noticed her, she froze, preparing. The instant she leapt, the bird took off.

"Poor Rayna," Tomás said, "she never gets the seagull."

"It's all right, she's had enough boar hunting to last a lifetime."

He kicked my boot. "That was your dream, not Rayna's."

I blushed, because technically he was right. Yet the more time that passed between the dream and the present, the more real the dream became for me. Now, a month later, the dream was nearly indistinguishable from my actual past.

"Also Rayna didn't die," he persisted.

"No, she didn't," I agreed, noticing how sad he looked. "That was your doing."

He frowned.

"It was your merciful God. I've been thinking about this. The Voice, Headache, they bring their aspect of being to whatever happens, good or bad. The cosmos is neutral. It's your God who cares what happens to us, because you chose a compassionate God."

"I didn't choose my God."

"Admit you prayed for Rayna to come home."

"Of course I did."

"There are many possible Gods, Tomás. Good for us you prayed to the merciful one."

He didn't even smile. "Lee, think about it. Rayna was out in the woods the whole time."

Oh no, he was a realist now? "Are you still arguing with God?"

He considered the stones at his feet. "No. God won that argument. I don't save people, he does."

But you do! I thought. "I've been holding out on you. It's important and I wanted to tell you in person."

He lifted his eyes curiously.

"You remember the night you flew to LA?" He nodded. "Did you dream?"

Snorting, he replied, "It was two stops. I never closed my eyes."

"Well that's too bad," I said casually, "because I was hoping we were in the same dream." He sat up to stare at me.

"You remember I told you how we all fell off the mesa together?" Even now, my pulse raced to think of it. "And Rayna and I split apart when we hit? I was as strong as I could be for her when she died, so she wouldn't worry. But it was unbearable. Then the Voice died, and I thought I'd go mad. When Headache crawled over to me, I wanted only one thing: to smash his head to pieces. I couldn't wait.

"I was crazy, I thought destroying him would make the world better. And I hated him so much, I wanted him to suffer. I threw a rock at him and it made a mess of his head, but he didn't die." I took a breath.

"I was looking for another rock to finish him off, when someone grabbed my arm. It was you, in a cassock of all things. You were so strong and kind, I threw my arms around you. I saw that you forgave me, and that's when I remembered how much I loved Rayna. I felt pure joy, the kind that comes from God."

Tomás was motionless.

"You understand what I'm telling you? If I killed Headache, goodness would have died in the world. You restored me, so I could carry her energy. You saved the world."

This time he smiled at the grandness of my words, and then put a hand to his face to wipe away tears. I knew he did understand. They were tears of relief, that he could return to who he was, and tears of gratitude, that God hadn't really left him.

Moved by affection, I put a hand on his shoulder and felt the dense muscular strength below his parka, so like Bill when he was forty. Sitting closer to this friend, I leaned into him with my arm on his back, and we gazed at the ocean as one person.

After a while he observed, "You know, you're different. You kept her energy."

What was he saying? Could I bring goodness to the world and give life to stars?

"That's ridiculous," I told him, "utterly impossible." But I knew, over the years, I would have to explore it. He was so often right about things like that.

We continued to sit together while Rayna tore across the beach, scattering a flock of seagulls that had the audacity to land.

Acknowledgments

When I started writing this book, I had only a premise, a few vague notions, and a question: would this premise turn into something worth reading? I wanted to discover the story as it developed, and I was very fortunate to have a willing group of early readers to let me know if the ideas were worth pursuing. I am indebted to all my early readers, especially Carolyn May, Kay Curtis, and Deborah Cotter, who gave me encouragement at every draft. Andrea Lucas, Cathy King, and Kaer Southard made valuable comments on the third draft, Roland Goodbody provided insightful copy editing, and Grace Peirce did the excellent book production.

Throughout, I used the internet to gather information on such diverse topics as canine vision, car skids, and brain anatomy, in order to ground the story in some form of reality. In particular, these internet articles gave me indispensable information:

Kai Ken - Excellence in a Classical Japanese Dog, written by Takuro Yanagisawa of Kai Ken Society Tokyo Branch, as translated by Nobuko Hasegawa Weeks. Copyright © 2017 NAKA. http://www.kai-ken.org/archive/excellence.htm

Suwannee River Ranch, year round wild boar hunting. http://www.suwanneeriverranch.com/

Last, I wish to thank the beautiful state of Maine for the opportunity to rearrange its locations, highways, and cellular coverage to suit the needs of the story.

Made in the USA
Middletown, DE
19 January 2020

83238932R00090